Get it Right

SKYE KILAEN

A LOVE AT KNOCKDOWN STORY

This is a work of fiction. Names, characters, places, and incidents either are the product of the author's imagination or are used fictitiously.

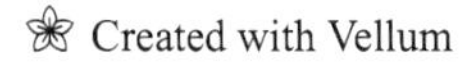

Created with Vellum

CONTENTS

ABOUT THIS BOOK

A butch lesbian parolee. The pretty pansexual nurse who got away. Is this their second chance at a happily ever after?

Finn is finally out of prison, which is great. Having no job, no car, and no place to sleep except her cousin's couch? Not so great. Plus, her felony theft conviction isn't doing wonders for her employment prospects, so she can't afford her migraine meds without the public clinic.

The last thing she ever expected was for the gal who stole her heart to come walking down that clinic's hallway: Vivi, the manicure-loving nurse who spent two years fighting the prison system to get proper medical care for her patients, including Finn.

Finn could never believe she imagined the attraction and affection between them. But acting on that in prison, especially as nurse and patient, had been a serious No Way. She's had eight months to get over Vivi, who abruptly left her job without saying goodbye. Finn is over it. Honest! It's totally and completely fine.

Except Vivi, here and now, doesn't seem fine. And Finn couldn't live with herself if she didn't try to help.

Is fate offering Finn a second chance? Or is finding love as likely as finding a job with health insurance?

CONTENT WARNINGS

I've tried to make these as spoiler-free as possible, but to me it's more important that folks who need content info can get it. If you don't need them, just skip this!

On-page / extensive:

- Sex (explicit in Chapter 9; less detailed reference in Chapter 14)
- Reflection on negative prison experiences, including delay of medical care and observing trans inmates being housed in wrong prison
- Reflection on factors that lead to people being in prison, including abuse, addiction, and poverty
- Housing insecurity and prospect of living with homophobic parents
- Difficulty accessing a prescription from a government-funded program
- Character with chronic migraines has one start on-page

- Unintended pregnancy with serious consideration of both abortion and continuing the pregnancy
- Vomiting
- Side character is a former police officer
- Phone call from an inebriated side character

Off-page or brief mention:

- Mentions of character's mother dying when she was a young child and parentification of oldest sister
- Descriptions of being rejected by parents for sexual orientation
- Recovery from injuries sustained in a car accident
- Weaning off pain medication
- Discussion of biological parent not being able to raise their child
- Character with young children has been abandoned by spouse
- Volunteering at abortion clinic (note: this is included only because some readers may have had stressful or dangerous experiences while volunteering)

Additional content warnings for sneak preview:

- Cheating by secondary character
- Interrupted sexual situation, non-detailed
- Use of dating app

PROLOGUE

"Finn? If you're awake, give me a sign."

That hushed voice wasn't the weekend nurse for the prison infirmary. It was Vivi. More officially, Nurse Curiel. That meant it was now Monday, which was fine by Finn. This weekend hadn't done her any favors. It was *fired*. No, wait. If it was Monday now, the weekend had already quit. Cool. Maybe she'd make a note in its permanent record anyway just in case.

Once she could open her eyes, if her eyelids would cooperate. They usually tried to go on strike after a bad migraine.

Finn tried turning her head and didn't much enjoy the feel of her neck and jaw. A hand caught the ice pack—well, used-to-be-ice pack, now room temperature—before it slipped off her forehead.

"Want to try water?" Vivi asked, still not too loud. She always kept it down until she knew Finn was okay. She kept the light off over Finn's bed, kept the guard from dragging the metal chairs across the tile which the jerk did even knowing they screeched. Vivi kept Finn safe, as best she could.

Finn managed to crack her eyes open. At first, she saw only blurs: Vivi's regulation blue scrubs and her lightly tanned face. The tan was a little unfair since it was only April, but Vivi tanned easily for a white gal. Finn and her lifelong history of sunburning her pale skin were occasionally jealous.

Blinking a few times added detail. Vivi and the staff appearance guidelines had a conflicted relationship, so her sunny red lipstick today was slightly too bold. Her long dark hair, though, was up in its usual inoffensively neat bun. The color on her short nails—only the most durable polish so it wouldn't chip at work—was similarly tame, the same shimmery pink she'd worn two weeks ago. *On a Thursday and Friday*, Finn's brain helpfully supplied, *right after the plum one with the glossy top coat.*

Finn told her brain to take a hike and reached up for the ice pack so Vivi could let go. Their hands brushed in the process. Finn tried not to enjoy it too much.

"Hey there." Finn's voice was rougher than she'd hoped it would be. She'd wanted to sound like a person, not a patient, and ugh, who knew what her hair was doing at this point? Finn might not be allowed her preferred style because of how the dang "extreme haircuts" policy was interpreted here, but she did still have some pride.

"Hey there yourself." Vivi beamed down at Finn as if her day had just gotten one hundred percent better.

Vivi gave her that smile often. It was the best part of Finn's days, or at least the normal weekdays, when Finn had volunteer duty in the infirmary instead of being laid up in it. An unpaid prison assignment was better than having nothing to do. The other two days of the week, Finn aimed to get through by keeping her head down, and most of the time it even worked.

Vivi pulled a rolling stool bedside, sat, and offered Finn a plastic cup of water. Finn propped herself up on the pillows, which sent the ice pack from the back of her neck sliding down. Their hands brushed yet again as Finn took the cup. Finn tried to ignore it, and she tried to ignore how lonely it felt watching Vivi trying to ignore it too, and they both sat silently while Finn took a sip through the straw and waited for her stomach to protest. It didn't. Cool.

"Finn, do I have to verbally kick someone's ass on your behalf?" Patient care failures were Vivi's nemesis, and when she found one, she was rarely inclined to leave it alone.

So Finn stalled. "What do the notes say?" It would have bordered on insubordinate if Finn had asked any other nurse, but Vivi Curiel wasn't any other nurse. She and Finn were coworkers, friends…

And it had to stop there.

Finn knew it, really she did. She was a prisoner, Vivi was staff, and the rules existed for a reason. It was scary when somebody with power got into a thing with somebody who had none. Finn had watched it happen to other prisoners.

"The notes claim," Vivi responded, starting to get a familiar steely glint in her eyes, "that per my explicit standing order, you received your meds within twenty minutes of asking the guard for them. But I believe the person who wrote those words about as far as I can throw the entire west wing of this building."

Vivi's anger was gratifying. At least one person in this concrete complex gave a damn about Finn's well-being. But what if that one person made too much fuss and she ended up out of a nursing job?

There'd be no more placing mental bets on which color polish Vivi would wear next. No more spirited debates about who to put on a super-team made up of kick-ass women from action movies. No more quiet confessions about growing up motherless, Vivi's mom passing away and Finn's mother abandoning her parenting duties to devote her life to her church. No more listening to Vivi's whispered emphatic speeches about underfunding of health care in the criminal justice system, the mass incarceration crisis in general, or the Texas Legislature's latest boneheaded decision that would only make things worse.

No more realizing they were standing a little too close, smiling a little too softly, and seeing the same thing Finn was feeling in Vivi's eyes before they both looked away.

"Don't worry about it." Finn forced herself to sit up more. Ordinarily she found Vivi's righteous indignation one of her more appealing qualities, but escalating this might not end well for either of them. "I'm serious. I'll schedule better next time."

Vivi's red lips twitched with amusement. "Schedule your migraines better?"

"Only on weekdays between six a.m. and four p.m. from now on. Scout's honor."

"You were a Girl Scout?" Vivi asked skeptically.

Finn did her best to grin. "You think I got this gay without doing a lot of camping?"

Vivi snickered and gave Finn a sarcastic thumbs up. Finn caught Vivi's hand playfully, purely on reflex.

It felt so right.

It was so wrong.

Vivi took her hand back immediately.

"Nurse Curiel?" the guard called from across the room. "Everything okay?"

Not good.

The nurse in question straightened her back and stood up. "Everything's fine," she called back. "Thank you."

They waited to see if the guard would pull himself up out of his chair and walk over all slow and menacing, as if he'd be plenty happy if Finn was starting something. He didn't, though. He simply rolled his eyes, re-crossed his arms, and went back to staring around the room.

Vivi turned her attention back to Finn. "That can't happen again," she said, her voice so low only the two of them could hear. Not reproachful or condescending. More… regretful.

Finn had undoubtedly spent way too much time imagining what Vivi would say to her if they could freeze time or step into an alternate universe or get teleported to another country, anything to let them step outside of their roles for five freakin' minutes. Just so Finn could take a full, deep breath and she and Vivi could be completely candid with each other for once. Would Vivi say *Finn, you're fooling yourself*? Would she say *Finn, even if things were different, it would never happen*?

Her gut said no. Not when Vivi looked at her exactly like this so often, as if Finn's touch would be welcome if only the circumstances *were* different. As if Vivi was stopping herself from leaning forward only because she knew stopping herself was the right thing to do.

It was, of course. Five magical minutes of honesty wouldn't change reality.

"I'm sorry." Finn didn't know if she was apologizing for the touch, or for being in prison in the first place, or both. What she'd done by putting herself here meant they'd found each other, but it also meant an uncrossable distance between them. Win-lose.

Vivi nodded. Then she nodded a second time, more briskly. Professional. "Can I please make noise about this med delay? You should be able to get treatment when I'm not here. You all should." She sounded so worn down, and it was only Monday.

"No need," Finn reassured her. If she could do nothing else, Finn could at least give Vivi a day without another fight.

Vivi didn't appear the least bit happy about acquiescing. "Okay, next question. Are you hoping to work today, or should I write you a slip?"

Because of course Finn would need a slip to miss a work shift in the prison infirmary due to being in the prison infirmary. Had the outside world been this ridiculous? Finn sat up. The floor needed mopping, clean linens needed bringing up from the laundry, beds needed changing. It gave her something to do beyond contemplating how thoroughly she'd screwed up her life. The room stayed clear despite the angry throb near her eye. Not bad enough to skip her shift.

Vivi must have seen her flinch, however. "Nope, you're in bed for today."

"Come on, I'll be fine."

"You have a nursing license too?" Vivi exclaimed, eyes wide. "You never told me! No, seriously, lie down."

Which was typical of how Vivi took care of her patients, though keeping prisoners in hospital beds didn't make her popular with some of the guards and admin staff. Hospital beds were more comfortable than regular bunks.

Vivi helped Finn ease back down, took the expired ice packs, and returned with two fresh ones before Finn had even snagged the sheet to pull it up. Vivi smoothed the blessed cold onto Finn's head in exactly the right places, took her pulse at the wrist, and covered her with the sheet.

All without a single unnecessary touch, because Vivi and ethics got along much better than Vivi and dress codes.

"Get some actual sleep," Vivi said gently. "When you wake up I'll tell you where I'm up to in The Last Airbender."

Finn's eyes drifted half closed. She was more worn out than she'd wanted to be. Tomorrow she'd double-time to get caught up. Vivi worked hard enough; she didn't need to pick up Finn's slack too. "You've forgiven me about the bats rushing out of the cave in that one episode?"

Vivi chuckled. "You'll be forgiven when my roommate forgives *me* for waking her up when I shrieked."

Finn gave her a sleepy thumbs up. "I accept full responsibility for not knowing you were afraid of bats, but it's a travesty you've never seen it all."

"Oh absolutely," Vivi said with mock seriousness. "I had all the time in the world for TV while getting my degree and working over twenty hours a week, and I made bad choices. I'm so glad you came along to get me sorted out."

Finn made an agreement-sounding hum; all she could manage. She should have gotten up. She could have. If Vivi had cleared her, she'd have made it through the day. She'd worked through worse at her last job, since it lacked paid sick days, a living wage, and management with any kind of morals.

However, Vivi had said to stay put, and now that Finn was lying back down, she had to admit her desire to get up was next to nil. It would be okay if she missed one more day to unconsciousness.

Two days later, when she walked into the infirmary and found a new day nurse in Vivienne Curiel's place, Finn sure as hell wished she'd made a different choice.

CHAPTER ONE

Nearly eight months later

Finn wouldn't have appreciated the exam room in the low income clinic half as much before prison. It might be shabby, but its walls had posters of kittens. Before prison, Finn would have noted those kittens in passing and moved on to stressing about something. Going to prison had left her with a lot less to stress about. No toxic job anymore. No on-again, off-again girlfriend either.

So there was plenty of space for enjoying the kittens. Her favorite was the black one with the white spot around its left eye. It looked a bit sassy, like a troublemaker, yet cute. You couldn't be mad if it climbed the curtains.

Finn had never had such detailed thoughts about kittens in her life as in this room, but it wasn't like she had anywhere else to be. An article she'd stumbled across had said to treat finding a job as a job itself and spend at least forty hours a week on it. The most Finn had hit in the three weeks and change since her release was thirty two. She suspected most of the postings she'd responded to were perpetual, meant to keep a slush pile in case of a vacancy. Few places were hiring for seasonal work in the couple of weeks before Christmas and New Year's; those jobs got filled before Black Friday... by people without felony theft convictions.

Two different nonprofit employment services had been a bust so far as well. Finn had gone so far as to email every business in the queer chamber of commerce listings, hoping she didn't sound desperate, requesting any leads on menial positions. When she'd asked her parole officer for ideas, he'd scanned her extensive log of work search activities and shrugged.

Would she be starting the new year employed? Signs pointed to no. Which sucked, but it wasn't a surprise. She'd find something eventually; it didn't have to be fantastic. The Austin bus system wasn't as bad as she'd feared, so she could forgo the expense of a car. A girlfriend could wait even longer. None of her romantic relationships before prison had been particularly inspiring, and the woman she'd felt the strongest connection with in her whole life had possibly been the worst case of *wrong place, wrong time* ever.

Finn had already spent approximately ten zillion too many wakeful hours wishing that situation had worked out differently. She'd never come up with a single way it could have without a natural disaster or alien abduction, neither of which would have been great. Probably.

Anyway, Finn was moving forward. She needed migraine meds, which she'd already put off getting for far too long, working her way through the Medical Assistance Program application process while hating having to ask for help. All she had to do now was sit in the exam room and speculate about the personalities of kittens until a doctor showed up.

A clinic nurse came in first, saving Finn from her feline-related thoughts. She apologized for running late, but why would Finn complain about free health care? She counted herself lucky to have gotten her appointment moved up, especially three days before Christmas. Thank goodness the person who'd answered the phone had believed Finn that *prodrome* meant *I'm going to have a migraine literally today, this can't wait.*

The nurse stayed for all of four minutes. Twenty minutes later, the doctor visited for five minutes, kind but harried. He agreed Finn needed both kinds of meds, the daily preventative she'd had the most luck with, and the abortive nasal spray for when the preventative didn't work. Or, like today, when it hadn't been available. Finn was assured her prescriptions would be e-zapped to the H-E-B grocery store on South Congress, and their pharmacy was open until nine o'clock. All she had to do was show her MAP card, and sweet, sweet lack of soul-crushing pain would (hopefully) be hers.

Finn said goodbye to the doctor and the kittens and stepped back out into the hall—

Only to see Vivienne Curiel walking towards her.

Even after eight months, Finn knew she couldn't be anyone else. Vivi's bun had lavender in it now, and was higher, almost on top of her head, and now her scrubs were hot pink instead of prison staff blue. She'd put on some weight and looked seriously va-va-voom. Vivi glanced up from the chart she'd been scanning and stopped short about five feet away, her lip-glossed mouth dropping open. She was as stunning as the day Finn had last seen her, the day Vivi had said a cheery goodbye as if everything was completely normal.

Finn waited to find out if Vivi would come closer, or turn around and go as if they'd never even known each other, as if they'd never been... whatever they had never been.

Vivi closed her mouth, made her decision, and walked to the open doorway Finn was blocking. Her voice came out higher than Finn remembered it. Nervous. “Finn? How did— Um, what are you doing here?”

Not the first words Finn had been hoping to hear. When she couldn’t stop herself daydreaming about running into Vivi somewhere, she’d envisioned something along the lines of *Finn, oh wow, how are you?* or *Thank goodness you’re free, take me home and cover me with kisses*.

Okay, not really the last one. That would be weird.

Finn held up her post-visit printout like an elementary school hall pass while she waited for her brain to reboot. She couldn’t stop staring at Vivi. There were dark circles under her eyes which Finn didn’t remember from before. Vivi was exhausted, or maybe sick. Also gorgeous and standing right here. Finn’s nervous system had no idea what to do with all this information.

“I guess you’re—” Vivi started, as Finn managed “Are you o—”

They both stopped.

This was weirder than the *cover me with kisses* vision. This was flat-out awkward. Why? They’d been friends first, whatever else either of them had wanted, and they hadn’t parted on bad terms. Finn had made the one regrettable slip near the end, holding Vivi’s hand, but she’d been forgiven. Hadn’t she?

“So you aren’t… here to see me?” Vivi asked.

Oh no. Finn could see it from Vivi’s perspective. Girl quits job, girl gets new job in Austin hundreds of miles away, then other girl from old job randomly appears at new workplace? Prison staff probably had to be careful about that kind of thing.

But whatever peace Finn had finally made with Vivi’s disappearance had come when she’d put the past behind her. Regardless, Finn never would have come to Vivi’s work uninvited. If Finn had learned anything from her prison stay, it was how much she'd taken privacy and boundaries for granted before.

Plus, this wasn't how Finn would have wanted a reunion to go. Too many of the questions Vivi might ask had awkward answers. Where was Finn working? Nowhere. Where was she living? In her cousin's stepsister's living room trying not to disturb any of the Christmas decorations, and yeah that was a damn long story.

"I didn't have a clue you worked here," Finn promised, relieved this was a misunderstanding and she hadn't unknowingly committed some transgression. There were enough in the known column already. "I didn't even know you lived in Austin now." Finn would have remembered any mention of Austin in Vivi's bio, since Finn had expected her cousin Hollis who lived here to put her up. Which he was doing as best he could.

Finn expected Vivi to relax now that Finn's presence had been explained. Instead, she hiked the patient chart up in front of her chest. When she spoke, she was obviously trying to be Nurse Curiel, but Finn could only give it a seven out of ten for verisimilitude. Too shaky.

"Oh." Vivi put on a smile Finn had only seen her use with strangers. "Well. I'm glad you're out, that's wonderful. If you have any questions later, call the nurse line, and if you don't get what you need there, ask for a call back from the nurse manager." She sounded like she was preparing to give Finn more instructions for if things went wrong, such as how to escalate to the Executive Director, or contact the media for an investigative report, but she visibly stopped herself. "I'm glad you're getting care. Maybe I'll run into you here again. Bye, Finn."

Finn might not have known Vivi lived in Austin now, but she knew something was wrong. “Vivi, wait. Please.”

Finn had never said Vivi’s name out loud. She’d only ever heard that nickname said by other staff at the prison. It must have been waiting on the tip of her tongue all this time, or *Nurse Curiel* would have come out. She kinda wanted to say it again, so she could hear it again in her own voice.

But Vivi had already turned back, listening. Finn’s eyes grabbed every detail she could. The freckles across Vivi’s nose and cheeks, darker now, especially the two above the corner of her lips. The shimmery eye shadow. The way her chin might be about to start trembling like on Vivi’s twenty-seventh birthday when she’d been missing her mother.

She wasn’t okay. Vivi wasn’t okay, and maybe Finn was at fault or maybe not, but either way Finn couldn’t stand it.

“Can we talk?” Finn tried to put all her genuine concern into the question and none of her selfish confusion. “Sometime? Catch up?”

Vivi didn’t immediately walk away, but she didn’t open up either. After a moment she seemed to pull up some reserve energy and gave Finn another smile. Still fake, though, as if Finn was no longer someone Vivi could turn to.

It stung.

“Sure,” Vivi said, a pale echo of her old cheery self. “We should catch up. Um… tonight? Is that too soon? Today I actually know I’m getting out of here on time. We could meet at Knockdown Coffee at six thirty?”

Finn didn’t have a clue where Knockdown Coffee was, but she’d get there even if she had to take a cab with the emergency cash her cousin had given her.

“Yeah. Sounds perfect.”

Vivi nodded sharply, all business. “See you there.”

Then Vivienne Curiel, the wrong place, wrong time

woman Finn hadn't been able to forget no matter how hard she tried, walked on down the hall.

Knockdown Coffee. Six thirty. Finn could totally do this. She'd pick up her pills, take one immediately, add just enough but not too much caffeine, and find a dark place to sit for a couple of hours while the worst of the oncoming brain storm passed her by.

Afterwards, hopefully, she'd find out what the heck was going on with Vivi.

CHAPTER TWO

Finn found Knockdown Coffee, which was flying a Pride flag outside, by six twenty. At least she hoped it was Knockdown Coffee. The beginnings of the migraine aura made it difficult to confirm by, well, reading the sign.

She could have read the sign if she'd gotten her pills. She might have gotten her pills if the pharmacy could have gotten the MAP office on the phone to verify her eligibility. Or if the cash she carried had been enough to say hell with it and buy them at the jaw-dropping prices without insurance. Alas, no. Now Finn had maybe an hour and change before she'd likely be out back in the alley puking up her guts.

She could make this work. All she had to do was stop gritting her teeth before she cracked one of them, which was not helped by the jingle bells clashing when she opened the door. Sounds like that always cut right through her brain. If they were seasonal, they were the only holiday decoration Finn could make out in the shop, which she would likely have found relaxing under less head-crushing conditions. Bold art on the walls, charmingly mismatched furniture, colorful stained concrete floor. Very quirky. Very South Austin.

The white barista behind the counter was short, with shoulder length blond hair held back by a blue bandana and what Finn thought were multiple piercings in both ears. He was so South Austin that Finn wondered if he ever went north of the river.

"Hello and welcome to Knockdown!" he called, smiling broadly as Finn approached. "You're new here, right? I'm Will Strauss, he/him. We do pronouns here, but you don't have to if it doesn't feel right. I'm one of the owners. Love your hair, by the way, super dashing!"

Finn's hand went up reflexively to the buzzed back of her head. Her cousin Hollis couldn't do as much for her as he wanted to right now aside from a bed, but on the first night after her bus trip to Austin he'd taken pity on her and fixed her hair. An undercut, jeans, her Docs, and her much-missed burgundy satin bomber jacket over a white v-neck t-shirt? So much better. The haircut might make job searching more difficult, but it had done a lot to make the Finn in the mirror look like somebody she recognized.

She wasn't the same, of course. She was twitchier than she used to be, and it was a hard gearshift to go from being watched all day without being seen, to being... well, invisible, she sometimes felt, moving through the city with nowhere to be and no one waiting for her. Therapy probably wouldn't be a terrible idea once she could afford it. First she had to get through the next few hours without making a spectacle of herself.

Finn thanked Will and gave him her coffee order. While he filled her cup and Finn tried not to rub her temple, a dark-haired white woman even taller than Finn's 5'10" came out from the back room and stared at her. At least Finn thought she was staring. Maybe she was just standing there. Either way, she was a solid gal and Finn did not want to meet her in a dark alley, especially if Finn had thrown up in it. She might need a new plan for later.

Will came back to the counter and handed Finn her coffee cup. He gently helped her steady it, even with one of his pinky fingers splinted as if he'd broken it. Finn couldn't tell if her own hand was shaking or she couldn't see the cup properly.

When Will seemed confident she had it, he let go and gazed up at the looming woman. "This is Nora. She's the love of my life as well as my business partner."

The woman may or may not have rolled her eyes lightly and snorted.

"Finn, she/her." Finn tried her best to step back from the counter without being rude. She had to sit down before she fell down. Or crawled under a table to curl up in a ball, which would attract attention she didn't need.

"Interesting," Nora said slowly.

Finn had no idea why her name and pronouns would be interesting.

The bells on the door behind her jingled again. Would it be so wrong to rip them down and melt them into slag? She needed to cut down the chat she wanted to have with Vivi. It probably boiled down to two things anyway: was Vivi okay, and could Finn help?

Of course, out of the two of them, who had a criminal record and fines and the fees she had to pay for her own parole out of a paycheck she didn't have? Who was sleeping on a relative's couch and spending most of her days in the public library? Not Vivi.

When Finn turned, however, she saw it *was* Vivi who'd set off the bells coming in.

"Little sister!" Nora called, a bit pointedly. "We were meeting Finn."

Little sister. Vivi had always been careful not to use names when she talked about her personal life, but now Finn could put the pieces together. The gal behind the counter was one of Vivienne's two older sisters, and her height made her the one who'd been a cop. Vivi had sent Finn to her sister's coffeeshop. Was today the most ridiculous Finn's life had ever been? *Scientists might never know for certain.*

"Back off," Vivi warned, and at first Finn assumed she was getting the beginning of a speech Vivi hadn't wanted to give at her workplace. Hadn't Finn already explained her showing up had been a coincidence? Then she realized Vivi was talking to Nora.

"Oh!" Will said brightly. "You're *that* Finn. Wow! Okay, let me wipe down a table for y'all. Can I get you sandwiches on the house? Nora, babe, can you get more napkins down off the top shelf?"

Nora grumbled her way into the back room. Will wiped down a table, dried it, brought them both water, tried and failed to talk Vivi and Finn into food, and gave Finn's shoulder a reassuring squeeze before he buzzed away back to the counter.

At least somebody was on her side? Why were there sides? Why did they know her name? Finn was too far out of it for this much interpersonal complication.

Once they were alone, Vivi studied Finn. "Are you okay?"

Finn smiled, going for sure and confident. "I'm fine." She took a sip of her coffee. The caffeine wouldn't fix anything at this point, but she was screwed either way and she liked warm beverages. Vivi was sitting across from her. Both of them in civilian clothes, Finn with a decent haircut, and nobody waiting for her to step back into a room full of bunk beds so they could lock her in with ten other women and the one trans guy being kept in the wrong prison because the correctional system was fucked up about that stuff.

Vivi wasn't buying the brushoff. "You've yawned three times since I walked in the door."

Finn shouldn't have been so touched that Vivi remembered her migraine tells. They'd been coworkers and friends for two years, apart from anything else, and Vivi was a nurse. "I'm good, but I'm worried about y—"

Vivi interrupted by pushing her chair back. "You used your abortive spray, right? I'll take you back to the office and we can turn off the lights until it kicks in. Come on."

Finn waved her hand in what she hoped was a blithe, unconcerned manner. "It's under control. Can we talk?"

Vivi rested her hands on the table. Shimmery lavender nails now. To match her hair? She'd changed out of her scrubs, into jeans and a drapey jewel-tone purple sweater, but she hadn't taken her hair down. Finn had always wanted to see Vivi's hair down. Not right now. Right now she wanted someone to hit her in the head with a brick to knock her out until the migraine ended. Or they could use a frying pan or a bowling ball, she wasn't picky.

"Finn?" From the way Vivi said it, Finn must have missed the first time. "Are you still using the same medications? May I see them?"

"Couldn't get them." The muscle tension on Finn's right side was now fighting her for control of her jaw. "MAP card didn't work."

Finn was mildly shocked Vivi *knew* some of the next words she said. She moved around behind Finn while cursing and dug her thumbs into the exact spot in Finn's right shoulder that always got it the worst. The damn bells went off again and Finn had to close her eyes.

It was possible this had not been one of her better ideas.

"I'll drive you home. Where are you living? I'll map it so you can keep your eyes closed."

"With Hollis," Finn said. "My cousin? On the couch. Can't go until after the kids go to bed.

"When did he have kids? Sorry, irrelevant right now. Can you get up?"

Finn heard Will asking Vivi if he and Nora could do anything, and Finn laughed despite her unsettled stomach. Probably all Nora wanted to give Finn was a drop kick away from Nora's baby sister.

"Help me get her to my car, I'm taking her to my place. Finn, come on, can you stand up?"

Finn had wanted to find out what was making Vivi seem so worn down. She had wanted to save the day. Instead she ended up staggering out of Knockdown with one arm over Vivi's shoulders and Will's arm around her waist from the other side.

Worst. Butch. Ever.

The colder air outside was better. Vivi, bless her, turned off her car stereo without Finn having to ask. Halfway there, Vivi pulled into a drugstore parking lot for Excedrin, which she said would be better than nothing. Finn had her doubts based on past experience, but she got it down with a sip of juice from a bottle Vivi held for her. She gave herself high marks for staggering all the way into Vivi's bathroom before she puked it back up. While she had her head over the toilet, she heard Vivi remark darkly that they could take turns.

Vivi had a stomach bug? No wonder she looked miserable. Finn throwing up wouldn't help; hearing other people throw up was gross in the best circumstances. Finn did her best to apologize between heaves.

"You're fine," Vivi said in her kindest voice, the one she used when someone was really hurting. Finn had been so achingly grateful for that voice the first time Vivi took care of her—for someone who gave a damn about how patients *felt*, not only whether she'd checked the right procedural boxes. "It's not your fault. I can get the med thing straightened out once you're okay on your own, with your permission."

Finn made an agreement noise and slumped down on the tile to appreciate the cold stability of it for a bit before she threw up again. Tile was so much better than carpet or prison concrete.

Vivi settled something soft over her. When had she left to get it? "This is washable," she promised, "so don't let me catch you worrying about getting it dirty. Rest when you can. I won't be far away, but here's one of my hairbrushes, toss it towards the doorway to get my attention. Right here there are two ice packs and some mint gum to smell."

It was literally everything that could possibly take the edge off without Finn having to ask. Vivi hadn't even turned on the bathroom light.

Finn was gonna do whatever it took to make it up to her. Tomorrow, though. Assuming she lived that long.

CHAPTER THREE

When tomorrow rolled around, however, Finn was in fact still alive, but Vivi was nowhere to be found.

Finn couldn't be entirely positive it *was* tomorrow. Once the migraine itself had eased its boot heel off her brain, she'd slid into postdrome fog and dizziness. Vivi had eventually gotten Finn off the bathroom floor and made up the couch. She'd also tacked up blankets to block the light from the living room windows.

Living room windows. Finn was in Vivi's apartment.

She had to take a moment to let it sink in. Of all the outcomes of walking into that clinic, she could never have predicted this. She sure as hell wouldn't have wanted it. Crash landing back into Vivi's life as a patient was not the right kind of dramatic entrance.

Finn had only caught a couple visuals of the apartment in a blur on the way in. Now she could see that Vivi's taste for pretty, when applied to home decor, ran to cuddly pillows and fluffy blankets and nubby curtains, all in soft colors. A clear acrylic box on the shelf underneath the coffee table held a couple dozen bottles of nail polish, plus emery boards and whatnot. It couldn't be Vivi's entire collection, as there weren't nearly enough glitter options for days off work. No sign of anyone living there but Vivi, from what Finn could see without snooping. No holiday decorations, either.

The contents of Finn's pockets lay in a sad little pile on the kitchen counter. Prepaid phone, black wallet. Her bag o' meds was there too. *Huh.* When Vivi had said she'd straighten it out, she hadn't meant making a quick professional call. She'd meant going to the pharmacy and getting the problem completely solved. Finn shouldn't have been surprised.

Her phone told her this was December 24th, near lunchtime, and Finn's stomach lurched. She'd missed a whole day? Thank goodness there were no missed calls, but Finn fumbled open her email hoping desperately she hadn't missed one about a job.

Nope. Nothing new in her inbox. *Ah well.*

She did have a reassuring text from Hollis, whom she vaguely remembered Vivi asking permission to call so he wouldn't be afraid Finn was dead in a ditch. Of course he might murderize her himself when he found out she hadn't called him to pay for the meds.

Anyway. It was Christmas Eve, meaning her second day in Vivi's apartment, which was disorienting. Had Vivi gone to work yesterday, or had she missed a day to babysit Finn while she sort-of-slept it off? The latter was an alarming thought.

Finn risked some of the sports drink she found in the fridge, and it stayed down. She was good to go. As she pulled on her jacket, however, she wondered how many more cuss words Vivi would use if she came home to find out her patient had checked out without authorization.

Not worth the risk.

If she was staying until Vivi got home, though, she

needed to eat. Maybe she could cook, and then Vivi would have leftovers? Finn browsed the fridge and pantry and found fixings for spaghetti. Her stomach responded okay to the smell of the garlic, surprisingly, so she got started.

As she was finishing up, she was startled to hear Vivi's key turn in the lock. The clinic must close early on Christmas Eve.

Vivi stepped inside, paled, dropped her purse, and covered her mouth and nose. She took several steps into the kitchen, accidentally hip-checked Finn on her way to the sink, and barely missed retching into the now-empty pasta strainer.

Didn't her clinic give her sick days? Finn was no expert, but it seemed backwards to have nurses come to work to give patients germs.

"Hey," Finn said carefully, when it seemed Vivi might be done. "Are you still sick? Can I get you anything?"

Vivi coughed and spit. "I'm fine. This is perfectly normal."

A tingle of a suspicion ran up Finn's spine. Throwing up suddenly was normal for only a few reasons, and last time Finn had checked, Vivi didn't also have migraines. Which left chemotherapy or—

"I'm pregnant," Vivi said. "Whoever called it *morning* sickness was a dirty liar."

The garlic spaghetti was given to the downstairs neighbor, an elderly gentleman with three adorable whippets in matching holiday themed t-shirts. Finn followed Vivi's directions to a box fan in her bedroom closet and set it up to air out the apartment. Vivi cleaned up in the bathroom and took refuge in a plastic deck chair on the small back porch, curled up into a miserable ball where there was enough sun to counteract the day's chill.

She wasn't looking at Finn, so Finn looked at her through the sliding glass door the way she'd wanted to every day since they'd met.

Vivi had pulled a black velour hoodie on over her scrubs and taken her hair down. It was straighter than Finn would have thought. The lavender made it look as though Vivi's dark locks had been dipped in a pool of color. It was lovely. All of her was lovely, from that silky long hair falling down her back, to her dainty ears with almost no lobe, to the curves of her shoulders. She'd told Finn about dislocating the right one. Not fun.

Vivi had more hip and backside now, and more belly. From what Vivi had muttered about how many weeks she'd put up with the nausea, before fleeing the kitchen, Finn didn't think it was pregnancy weight yet. If it hadn't been for the something's-wrong vibe, Finn would probably have assumed this was Vivi's body when she was happier, that she'd found a better place for herself. As much as it had wounded Finn when Vivi left, the prison job had been too much pushing back against people who should be colleagues, or defending her professional decisions, or begging for supplies. Finn had known Vivi wasn't happy there.

And Finn *wanted* Vivi to be happy. She wanted Vivi joyful, laughing, or scrunching up her freckled nose like she did when something delighted her. If things had been different, Finn would have also wanted to talk long-running animated television series with her, see the rest of her nail polish collection, and find out what exactly Vivi had said about Finn to her family.

Maybe she could have held Vivi's hand, for real this time, without it being wrong or dangerous. Maybe she could have finally asked the question, out loud, without fear of anybody overhearing and without it being ethically screwed up:

Do you want this?

Unfortunately for Finn, she'd done plenty of thinking while she cleaned up the food, and she couldn't see any way that qualified as a good idea. Vivi was pregnant. Finn wasn't asking how it had come about; that was Vivi's to disclose or not. Regardless, it was clearly kicking her ass, and putting Vivi on the spot with a confession of romantic feelings didn't seem like a kindness.

Maybe there would never be a right time for them. Maybe the way they'd started was the way they'd go on, coming in and out of each other's lives only when all signs pointed to *not now* and *not like this*. It didn't stop Finn from worrying about Vivi needing help, though, and Vivi hadn't yet asked her to leave.

Finn went to the sliding door. When she stepped out onto the balcony, Vivi uncurled. She seemed better, but not great. Finn settled in the plastic chair across from her, kind of regretting not grabbing her jacket.

"So," she said, hoping levity might normalize things a bit, "if you left to join the witness protection program, you should probably ask to speak to a manager. You're supposed to at least get a new *name*."

Vivi stared at her in apparent confusion, then started to snicker. The snicker turned into a burst of laughter, and another, and she put down her glass of ginger ale on the little side table so she could cover her face and let herself go. Finn leaned back with a feeling of satisfaction. This she could offer, if nothing else.

When Vivi had mostly gotten herself back together again, she pointed one mock-accusing finger at Finn. "I should have known you could make me laugh right now." She wiped her eyes, choking down another giggle.

"So it's a good thing you rescued me from public humiliation?" It was out of her mouth before Finn had time to regret it. How would it feel if Vivi said no, or looked as though she wanted to?

Vivi rolled her eyes. "Oh stop! Nobody in there would have judged you for being sick. If they did, Nora would have kicked them to the curb."

On principle, maybe, not for Finn's personal sake. Or maybe that was too harsh. Finn had been in Nora's presence for all of three minutes, during an impending migraine. Not the best time for a first impression.

"Also, I'm so sorry," Vivi went on. "I sent you there without warning you it was Will and Nora's place. I run out of brain near the end of my shift now for anything outside of my patients, and it honestly never occurred to me to think that through."

"Don't worry about it." Would Finn have preferred a heads up? Sure. Had anyone taken her head off? Not literally. "Did they find better health insurance?" That problem was the last news Finn recalled hearing about Vivi's sister and her pansexual partner.

Vivi let out a long sigh. "Kinda? They got a cheaper plan through some small business association, but their coverage is terrible, and you know how Will is."

Accident-prone, she meant; Finn remembered the stories. Of course Vivi would worry about him and her big sister. When Vivi was little, Nora had practically raised her and their sister Alicia for a handful of years after their mom died. Whatever Vivi's frustrations about how Nora kept trying to parent her even in adulthood, which Finn had heard all about, they were close.

Vivi shifted in her chair and gazed down at her black and pink sneakers. The awkwardness between them certainly hadn't resolved itself with one joke.

Finn couldn't keep from asking any longer. "What happened? I showed up to work and you were gone." She hadn't meant it to sound so sad. She'd come out here to find out what *Vivi* needed.

Vivi gave her a small, tired smile. "You asked me not to complain about your last migraine so I didn't—cross my heart—but if you put any money on my big mouth eventually getting me fired, you can collect. When they got two qualified applicants for the other open position, I was out the door."

It fit. After the shock of Vivi's disappearance had worn off, Finn had reassured herself Vivi being fired was the most likely explanation. Some people who worked in the prison system were good, but it was a system, and systems want to run smoothly more than anything else. Vivi had consistently chosen patient care over smooth.

Plus, it would have left too deep a mark to believe Vivi had left voluntarily without saying goodbye. Finn would've had to admit she'd imagined even their friendship, let alone anything else she'd believed they shared.

"I'm sorry," Finn offered. It must have hurt being dismissed for caring too much.

Vivi shrugged. "I was pretty pissed off about it until I made the mistake of coming out to my father after Nora warned me not to. Then I had my father being a bigoted asshole to be mad about instead. There's only so many hours in the day, you know?"

Finn tried not to crack a smile. Nora warning her not to was probably half of why Vivi had done it.

"Of course she was right," Vivi continued, "so that was

annoying. I was staying with him and my stepmom after I moved back here, until my apartment was ready. So my timing was horrible, but he had the news on and made a nasty comment and it just... jumped out. I said bi instead of pan, since to me personally it's close enough and he'd know what it meant. He went off with almost half an hour of stereotypes and religious condemnation like he had a biphobia bingo card until I wanted to throw a chair through a window.

"He told me to get out, so I packed and sat on the couch loudly until Alicia and Matt called me back and said I could use their guest room. Sorry, that's my other sister and her partner, the pediatrician, you remember them?"

Finn nodded. Alicia. Matt. More people important to Vivi whom Finn knew so much about without having known their names. Finn sent grateful thoughts to those two for being there when Vivi needed someone. "I'm so sorry."

Vivi took another sip of her ginger ale. "Thanks. My stepmom's been great about it, so that's a bright spot. I think she's going to keep Dad from ruining Christmas for everybody. Unless Alicia decides to come out, too, in the middle of dinner, which I wouldn't put past her. She'd probably throw in that she and Matt have an open relationship and the whole house would explode. If you see smoke from South Austin— Oh. Wait." Her eyes went wide, concerned. "Are you going to be with Hollis tomorrow? Or do you have somewhere else to be? I know you're not religious but..."

"You're not either, last time I checked."

Vivi made a face. "Don't tell my parents. Seriously, you have somewhere to go, right?"

At least Finn could reassure her on that front. "Yep, tomorrow's family day for me too. Hollis's parents are driving in from Wimberley. We'll do a thing." Hopefully everyone would avoid talk about Finn's last few years, and also her right now.

"Excellent." Vivi sounded relieved. "So are you done, or on parole? Do you need any community services referrals? The clinic social worker can help you out."

Finn took a swig of her drink. She didn't want to veer back this direction. "I got out after Thanksgiving, and yep, it's parole. Hollis is graciously providing room and board until I can get back on my feet, so I'm all set." It was close enough to the truth. "How are things with you?"

Vivi wasn't deterred. "Room and board, except you said you're sleeping on a couch? How are you supposed to manage your migraines under those conditions? You told me he got a two bedroom condo."

A lot had happened since then. "He's on leave right now for health reasons and he sublet his condo to a visiting professor for the academic year, so we're both staying with his stepsister."

"His sister's name is Ilsa, right?"

Finn was oddly pleased by Vivi remembering the small detail. "Yep. They both have a lot going on, but it's working fine. I'm lucky."

Vivi continued to frown, but she didn't press the issue.

Which was better, because the full story was too much for this conversation. Hollis's accident, and Ilsa's husband having bailed on her not a week before it. Finn didn't know Ilsa too well. Finn had grown up with Hollis in the role of big brother, but Ilsa hadn't shown up until after Hollis's mom moved them to New Mexico. Now Finn was living in Ilsa's house, which was admittedly more precarious than staying with Hollis, but Finn was trying not to think about that since it was truly way better than nothing.

She was also trying to make up for imposing. She'd

offered to babysit, but Ilsa seemed to need Finn to just stay out of the way. So every evening when Finn let herself back into the house, she washed and folded kiddo laundry and quietly turned the kitchen from a three-kid disaster into a clean workspace ready for the next day. She did other chores when she could, but even with driving Hollis to physical therapy a couple times a week in his new car it didn't seem like enough.

"How's the job hunt going?" Vivi asked. "This isn't a great time of year for it, is it?"

More of exactly what Finn didn't want to talk about, either with Vivi or at Christmas dinner tomorrow. "I'll figure it out."

The odds weren't in her favor. Finn had looked them up on the internet like a person who wanted to be despondent. Unlike most of the people she'd been in prison with, she'd had advantages in life. White skin. An associate's degree, which didn't count to a lot of employers, but was better than nothing. No abuse history, no addictions, no mental illness. Those factors were still on her side, though the felony conviction made for a damn big stumbling block for the next seven or eight years until her conviction would expire from her background check under Texas law.

If she hadn't wanted this uphill fight, however, she should have made different choices. All she could do was try to get her life back on track. While she tackled that project, one thing she did have was time, and maybe Vivi needed some of it.

"If you need any help with anything, let me know," Finn offered. "If you're having a rough time and you need somebody to clean, or run errands, I've found myself with a flexible schedule." Hollis had offered to lend her his car. She could accept it for this.

Vivi squeezed her eyes shut, not at all the reaction Finn had been hoping for. She waited. Waited some more.

"I'm glad we ran into each other," Vivi said, opening her eyes and meeting Finn's. "You probably don't know how much you kept my spirits up those two years. So if anything goes wrong with your coverage again, please get a hold of me at the clinic. But— You wanted to get caught up. That's what you said. We're caught up now. Which is great." She smiled, but only a bit. "Unless there's something else?"

That wasn't a no to the offer of Finn's time. It also wasn't a yes. Finn couldn't tell if it was a boundary or what. After she'd pressed Vivi into meeting up in the first place, best to be clear.

"I don't have an ulterior motive," Finn reassured her, "but I'm around. What are friends for, right?" Damn, if it wasn't the most cliché thing she'd ever said, Finn didn't want to remember what beat it.

It didn't seem to make Vivi feel one bit better, either, judging by how she glanced away. Made sense. Finn was a former prisoner, a former patient, and she had $50 in her pocket only because her cousin had put it there. Reasonable people would wonder how long it would be before *let me help you* turned into *can I sleep on your couch, it's just for a few days?*

Especially because Finn had just slept on Vivi's couch for two days.

"I need this to stop here," Vivi said quietly. "Good luck, Finn. I really hope things go well for you."

Oh.

"Okay," Finn said, because her mouth needed to say something. "Cool. Sure. Thanks. You too."

Turned out being the one to leave wasn't any easier than being the one who got left. At least this time she knew why;

Vivi was asking her to go. The why behind it, whether it lined up with Finn's guesses or not, didn't much matter.

"Is it okay if I don't walk you to the door?" Vivi asked hesitantly. "The smell."

Finn nodded.

"You can turn the doorknob thing and it will lock behind you."

Finn nodded again. "Perfect. I'll do that."

She went inside and collected her phone, her keys, and her medications before heading towards the door.

Halfway there, she paused and glanced back. Vivi was still staring the opposite direction, maybe lost in thought, maybe not wanting to give Finn any encouragement.

Either way, it meant Finn could pop back to the kitchen island and leave a note with her number. Vivi probably wouldn't use it because she had people. But Finn would feel better knowing she'd left it.

CHAPTER FOUR

The house was dark upstairs by the time Finn let herself in. From the front hall where she left her Docs, she could tell the Christmas tree lights had been turned off too. Hollis sat on the living room couch, however, grey-faced under his scraggly lack of regular shaving.

He was hurting.

She should have come straight back to help keep three amped up kids from splattering the walls with icing and sprinkles. She'd meant to, but after leaving Vivi's apartment she'd needed time to settle and give her heart a talking-to, now she knew how their story ended.

"How long before you can have the next pill?" Finn asked, sitting down on the couch carefully so she didn't jostle him.

"At nine," Hollis said weakly. "I'm up to ten hours now. I could have skipped it and gone to bed if I hadn't picked up one of the twins this morning."

Finn studied her cousin more closely. Hollis had always been thin, but he'd crossed the line to gaunt now. His long light blond hair, same color as hers, was always in a messy ponytail these days, all flyaways and split ends. His brown eyes were still sharp when the medications let them be, but he had a ways to go yet getting back to himself. Finn remembered watching him catch a Frisbee in the park when he'd visited her in Fort Worth, both oblivious that she'd be arrested five days later. He'd made several leaps she'd sworn had cheated physics. Now he had to be careful turning to look at her lest he anger the back muscle gods.

"Please stop scrutinizing me," he said with a grim smile. "Where the heck have you been, and who was the woman who called and scared the heck out of me?"

Finn flinched. "Sorry."

Hollis waved it off. "She started by saying you were fine, so that helped while I was restarting my heart from hearing someone else's voice from your number. I didn't know you had any friends in Austin."

Finn settled back and ran her hand through her hair. "I didn't either." No one she knew from Fort Worth had ever moved to Austin because the rents were too high. Which meant it sucked she was starting over here, but there'd been nowhere else to go. "I went to my doctor's appointment and I ran into one of the nurses from the prison."

"Too bad it wasn't that Victoria," Hollis said. "You could find out where she disappeared to."

Funny you should mention. "Vivienne," Finn corrected him, but gently. He was stepping down the pain pills, but he didn't sleep well. "That's who called you."

Hollis was visibly taken aback. "Oh wow. Sorry. She didn't say she was a nurse or I might have put it together."

"Well who would have thought?" Finn reassured him. "Total coincidence. She and I went for coffee to catch up, except I ended up doing the head explosion thing and I didn't want to bust in on y'all with that. The good news is, I have both my meds now." Hopefully he wouldn't ask any questions. He had enough to manage without fussing over her already-resolved medication gap.

Hollis smoothed his hands over his thighs, a nervous gesture. He wore sweatpants these days instead of skinny jeans, loose t-shirts instead of fitted button downs. "I'm so sorry things are like this."

"Knock it off. Compared to almost anybody else getting out of there, I'm living a life of luxury. My only concern is not leaning on you for too much longer." Then she'd start paying him back for everything, starting with the shocking amount he'd paid to break her pre-prison lease so she wouldn't have an eviction on her credit report.

Hollis did the little hand tilt he'd taken up as the replacement for a shrug. "It'll take as long as it takes. Anyway, you found your mystery woman. Did you find out what happened?"

Yeah, she had, but Vivi had no interest in resuming even their friendship. However, Finn could answer Hollis's question, which was some kind of closure. "She got fired, basically for caring too much."

"You kind of suspected, yes? Or did I remember it wrong?"

Finn rested her head on the back of the couch. "You didn't. Not everybody working there was evil, but Vivi was the nail that stuck up the most."

"Whole system's poison," Hollis said through a yawn. "Could tell that much from your letters. So she took you home, nursed you back to health, you confessed your adoration, and?"

Surely the man could watch a soap opera if he needed romantic drama. Finn didn't have any. "Nothing of the sort. She's a nurse, I'm a former patient."

"Emphasis on the former, and you had a crush on her."

"Totally irrelevant."

"She took you home, Finn. She could have asked me to come pick you up."

"You can't drive yet."

"But did she know that?" Hollis asked as if it was a gotcha.

"You're professoring in psychology now?"

Hollis's face froze and Finn wanted to smack herself on the back of the head repeatedly. She lightly shoved his knee instead. "You're on medical leave. You'll get back to your bio majors soon enough, Dr. Lind."

If he didn't, at least he had the settlement from the accident. Finn hadn't expected it to be resolved so quickly, but Hollis's insurance company had torn up the trucking company whose driver had slammed into his small car. If Finn ever had a vehicle again, she was signing up with them.

"Tell me when it's nine, okay?"

Finn's heart went all ouch and she turned to face him better. "Twenty-three minutes left, Holl. You want ice? Heat pack?"

"Just keep me distracted. It's not too bad, but I don't want Mom and Grant seeing me either drugged up or worn out tomorrow. They've spent too much time worrying already."

So that was the impetus to taper off the pills. Maybe after Aunt Priscilla had departed, Hollis would be kinder to himself.

A problem for tomorrow. Right now, he needed distraction. "Here's something I haven't told you about working in the prison infirmary. I wasn't allowed to unpack boxes of wooden tongue depressors and put them in the cabinet. I couldn't handle medications, that makes sense. No sharp instruments? Obviously. But the tongue depressor thing?"

Hollis gave her a small grin, playing along. "You could sharpen them."

"Well sure, but whenever I imagined getting my hands on one of them, all I could picture was a diagnostic rampage making people say 'ahhh' and triggering their gag reflexes. Which would have made me unpopular, but what would they charge me with? Assault? Practicing medicine without a license? Both?"

"Finn."

"What?"

"You like the girl."

Finn blew out a breath. She was doing her best to bury that way down where it belonged. Had already begun to while talking with Vivi, or maybe she hadn't and the reason Vivi had pulled away was hearts showing in Finn's eyes.

Maybe if they'd had less time together, Finn would have had an easier time putting those hearts away in the first place, when Vivi had disappeared. She could have lied to herself that it was a passing crush. But they'd had two years of thirty hours a week, minus the too few days Vivi had taken off for vacation.

Working with someone for so long, you saw them. You knew which of their habits might annoy the heck out of you long term, such as cracking their knuckles multiple times an hour, or obsessively correcting people's grammar when the speaker's meaning was perfectly clear. You found out about their deep-seated attitudes from how they behaved. You saw how they treated people who had less power, and how they treated people who had more. The important stuff.

Finn liked all the important stuff about Vivi.

At first Finn had interpreted that warmth as coworker feelings, then good friend feelings. When she'd fallen for someone romantically before, it had been a rush, fast and bubbly. With Vivi it had snuck up on her, slow and sweet and comfortable, and by the time Finn had realized what had happened, it had been all around her.

"Yeah," she finally admitted, because Hollis wouldn't stop staring at her. "I like the girl. Honestly though, Holl, it doesn't matter."

That was one hundred percent the truth. She couldn't flip a switch and turn it off, but romantic feelings weren't mandatory assignments. Her irrelevant affection would sort itself out eventually unless she kept feeding it. That had been Finn's hard realization as she nursed one cup of decaf tea in a random coffee shop this afternoon while watching other people hurry home for Christmas Eve. She had to start letting go.

Hollis lifted an eyebrow. "Did you say anything? Ever? Did y'all talk about it before she left?"

Her cousin didn't understand prison. "Nope."

"Tell her now! It doesn't have to be a big deal. You could drop a comment about how you always had a thing for her and see how she reacts."

Finn shook her head. "You realize by your own logic that's basically lying, the past tense?"

He reached his hand out for hers, a silent apology in case he'd overstepped. She took it.

"You're right, my phrasing was fucked. But look, kiddo, I'm just saying life can change drastically at any time. Don't jump to conclusions and miss out on something special, okay?"

A solid general point, but its applicability to the Vivi situation was approximately zero. "Let me get your pill?"

Hollis nodded and sighed, letting her out of the conversation.

Finn headed to the kitchen. It was a disaster. Probably just as well, as it would give her something to think about tonight aside from Vivi, and then time would take care of her feelings eventually. Chances were Finn would never see her again anyway unless they crossed paths briefly in the hall at the clinic. Which was okay.

It had to be.

CHAPTER FIVE

The tree was lit up. Stockings had been emptied. The children were done tearing up wrapping paper and had moved on to playing with boxes, and sometimes even the presents that had come in them.

Finn wished they would have done the grownups' presents at the same time as the kids' ones, so that part would be over already too.

"Merry Christmas, Finn. This is from me and Grant." Aunt Priscilla handed her a green envelope with a spangly bit of ribbon attached to it. From the thickness of it, Finn could tell it had a gift card inside. So had the one Hollis had given her, and the one from Ilsa.

"Thanks." The word was tough to get out. Not because she was ungrateful, but because she hadn't wanted anything in the first place, and she *really* hadn't wanted any of them to feel obligated to bail her out. Not her Aunt Priscilla and Ilsa's dad, not Hollis, and definitely not Ilsa herself. They'd all already done enough for Finn without gift cards to Old Navy and Target, the kinds of places you could get, say, work clothes or new socks or any of the other basics Finn could buy for herself if she hadn't messed up her own life.

Finn opened the envelope, read the card with Priscilla's and Grant's signatures, and did her best to squelch any negative thoughts about the Bed Bath and Beyond gift card. Surely someday she'd have a bed or a bath again. And hey, it was more cheerful than getting money deposited in her prison commissary account, right?

"Merry Christmas," Hollis said to his mother, handing her a box wrapped with one of the three kinds of paper he and Finn had used to wrap all the household presents while Ilsa had taken the kids to a movie. "It's from me and Finn."

Not true. Hollis had put her name on it. She hadn't asked him to, hadn't known he'd done it until it was already done. She'd wanted to ask him to take it off but making a thing about it felt weird.

Everything felt weird. Christmas hadn't been an important holiday to Finn personally in a long time, but a lot of her family and friends had always made a big thing about it, and she'd been happy to go along.

Today, for whatever reason, all she wanted to do was hide in Hollis's room upstairs. The black mood wasn't going to get any better if she nursed it, however, and if she'd said she was sick, people would have kept coming to check on her. So here she sat watching Aunt Priscilla unfold tissue paper to reveal a gauzy cream scarf with butterflies on it.

"It's lovely," she said to Hollis, and then turned to Finn. "Thank y'all both so much."

"What a wonderful day," Grant said to Ilsa, who perched on the edge of the couch, one eye on the twins. "The tree is gorgeous, lunch was fantastic. Thanks for having us."

"I'm so glad we can all be together." Aunt Priscilla took

Hollis's hand. "What a year, right? Reminds you what matters."

It had been quite a year. Bad things had happened to Ilsa and Hollis. Finn, on the other hand, had been fortunate enough to depart prison, yet here she was feeling awkward and antisocial.

"New year, new start," Grant pronounced. "Speaking of which, how's the job search coming, Finn? Tough month for it."

Finn called up her old cashier smile. "Just gotta keep at it."

"Good attitude." Grant nodded approvingly. "Can't win if you don't play the game. Same goes for Hollis here in the dating department, am I right?"

Aunt Priscilla rolled her eyes. "Grant, he's got enough on his plate right now. Holl, I don't blame you one bit for needing time after that *Colton*." She said the name like an insult.

It was a name Finn had never heard before. "Who's Colton?"

"Someone whose ass I will thoroughly kick if I ever see him again," Priscilla said darkly.

Hollis shifted uneasily on the couch next to Finn. "Someone who doesn't matter. Ilsa, remind me how many kinds of pie we ended up with?"

"Four," Ilsa said. "Dad, apple pie for you, with ice cream?"

Grant stood up. "I'll come get it. You've all done enough."

Except Finn hadn't, really, aside from the gift wrapping, because Ilsa had kept telling her *Relax, enjoy, you're a guest.* As if Finn wasn't a guest every day with no end in sight.

Priscilla followed Ilsa and Grant, and Hollis trailed after

them. He probably thought she was mad. An ex-boyfriend everyone knew about but Finn? What the heck? But she wasn't mad. She was… fuck, who knew? Tired, even without much reason to be given her lack of employment.

Also, she probably had to admit, sad. The gal who got away had been located, and she didn't want anything to do with Finn.

The self-pity train was about to jump the tracks and smash several small buildings. Time to shake it off. Finn got up and headed not to the kitchen, but to the screened back porch for some fresh air.

Which turned out to be *cold* fresh air. The temperature had dropped 15 degrees since the day before. Finn relocated a headless Barbie from one of the wicker chairs and sat down. She'd done an hour of work search this morning before the kids got up. Maybe she should go up to Hollis's computer and do more. Nobody was updating online job postings on Christmas Day, but maybe she'd think of different search terms.

"I wish either of us had liked smoking," Hollis said behind her, amused. "We could share a cigarette on the back steps."

Finn had to laugh. They'd tried smoking only once, when Hollis was 15 and she was 11, a year before his family moved to Las Vegas. They'd both coughed enough to dissuade them from ever trying it again.

"Anything I can do in there?" Maybe if Finn could pitch in, it would get her out of this mess in her head.

"Let Ilsa run her show," Hollis said gently. "You don't look so great anyway."

Finn could have made a joke: Hollis was the one giving her haircuts these days, so whose fault was that? She didn't have the energy. "Why didn't you tell me about Colton?" She hoped she didn't sound like a sullen teenager, but the odds weren't favorable.

Hollis made a *hmmm* sound. "It hadn't been going on long enough to be serious. When I got hurt, Mom called him and he made it clear he hadn't signed up for the ICU. I'm surprised she didn't mention it when y'all had the phone call about the accident. She was so pissed."

Finn could well imagine. Aunt Priscilla had always gone to the mat for Hollis. Bisexual son? No problem, and nobody better mess with her kid. Finn had spent as much time at their house as possible once she'd realized she'd have to come out someday too and the reception at her house wouldn't be as warm.

Like what had happened with Vivi and her father. Finn could have been there for her.

For crying out loud, Ellen Amanda Finnegan, get it together!

"It's old news anyway," Hollis assured her. "I'm over it, and you're sitting out here when all the pie is inside. Ready to come in?"

Not if she was going to stay so dang maudlin and bring everybody down. "I'll be there soon."

Hollis sighed, but patted her shoulder before he went back in the house.

She had to kick this. She'd known the score when she got out—depending on others, no place of her own—and she was hella lucky to have this much. She'd *known* how it was going to be. But deep down she must have expected it to be different.

Especially seeing Vivi again.

Finn hadn't sought her out. She could have. With Vivi's name being so distinctive, it would have been easy. The first time Finn connected to the internet without anyone monitoring her activity, she could have found Vivi and left a comment on a social media profile or something. Thanked her, the way she would have on Vivi's last day at work if Finn had known it was her last day.

There was a reason she hadn't searched. Finn hadn't wanted to, not while she was playing the part of Hollis's overgrown kid sister, crashing on a couch that wasn't even his. The universe had brought Vivi across her path anyway when Finn didn't have a job, or a life really. She wasn't doing *anything*. She was just… waiting.

Finn wouldn't look down on anybody else for being jobless. Nobody's worth was defined by their employment status. That absence of judgment was so easy to apply to others, especially on a day of kids' presents and gift cards and missing years of Hollis's life and not being needed. Not by Ilsa, not by the business owners and operators of Austin, Texas. Not by Vivi.

Who could blame the gal? Vivi was in the world of employed people with apartments. Finn might as well be on the moon in comparison.

Luckily, there was still pie when Finn gave up and went back into the house: apple, pecan, and coconut cream. There was Blue Bell vanilla bean ice cream for the apple pie, the same flavor Finn and Hollis's grandma had served on special occasions, so Finn's decision on which pie was easy.

Aunt Priscilla cornered her in the kitchen before she could cut a piece.

"Hang in there," she said, taking Finn's hand and giving it a squeeze. "I'm going to ask around again once we get clear of the holidays, try to find you something. Part time would help, at least? Or temp work?"

Finn didn't trust herself to speak, given what her throat was doing.

"And don't worry about when Ilsa starts needing her space back. We can put you up for a few weeks, or maybe we can all chip in if you can find somebody renting out a room here in town. We'll work it out. You don't have to go to your mom and dad's."

Aunt Priscilla gave Finn's hand another squeeze and stepped out to intervene in a toddler knock-down drag-out.

Finn had somehow never realized her situation could get so much worse.

She abandoned the pie idea, headed up the stairs into Hollis's bedroom, closed the door, and paced. She'd rather sleep under a bridge than stay with her parents, stuck an hour and a half up the highway in Waco with no car. But if Hollis and Priscilla thought Finn was going to try bridge life, they absolutely would try to pay her rent somewhere else just like Priscilla said. Finn felt bad enough with Hollis paying for her share of the groceries. Rent was five or six times worse, easy.

Which meant her parents' house was now an option, because she'd rather get prayed over every day than burn through more of Hollis and Priscilla's money. Finn wasn't a teenager anymore. She could ignore her mother. Barring that, she could go for extremely long walks.

Finn flopped down on Hollis's bed. She'd known Ilsa wouldn't want her in the living room forever. In the back of her mind, she'd figured Hollis would move back into his condo in the summer, and if Finn was still unemployed, at least she'd be sleeping on *his* couch. If Priscilla expected Ilsa's hospitality to last until summer, however, she wouldn't have brought it up now.

Finn had to figure out another option. She'd sold plasma before to pay a bill here and there. The only reason she hadn't done it lately was the high likelihood Hollis would throw a fit. Payments for plasma wouldn't touch rent in Austin, though.

Her phone buzzed in her pocket. It was probably spam. Who would be texting her about anything important on Christmas Day? Her dad had called early in the morning for a couple minutes, but everyone else who might want to talk to her today was in this house. Oh. It could be Hollis, who'd texted her before when he needed something and he was too tired to take the stairs. Finn fished her phone out.

I'm sorry, Vivi's text said. *I shouldn't have shut you out. Can you meet me at Knockdown tomorrow evening and we can try again? I could use a friend right now if I didn't ruin everything. If I did I'm so sorry and please don't avoid the clinic I will stay out of your way.*

Finn hadn't answered a text so fast in her life. *No apology needed. Happy to meet. Hope you're okay.*

Not really. Thanks tho. 6pm?

A second chance. A third chance? Whatever the numbering system, Finn knew what she had to do. She might not have a clue what to do about housing, but maybe she could patch things up with Vivi.

I'll be there.

CHAPTER SIX

The day after Christmas, Finn pushed open the door of Knockdown Coffee for a second time. They hadn't taken down the bells, but today there wasn't a looming Nora. Instead, behind the counter, a hip-looking white guy with short turquoise hair in a blue apron with a bi pride pin on it poured a bright purple smoothie into an oversized pint glass. That was a lot of colors.

"Hi!" he said, less exuberant than Will, but friendly. "I'm Oliver, he/him. Been here before?"

"She has!" Will said as he stepped through the curtain. "Hey Finn! What are you having? Oh hey Ollie, I bet I know who that's for. What name did she put on it this time?"

Finn thought Oliver colored a little bit as he put the smoothie down carefully on the counter and called out, "Smoothie for Leia?"

The customer in question, a blonde with some pink streaks in her hair, got up from behind her fancy sticker-covered laptop and took off her expensive-looking noise-canceling headphones before coming to the counter for her drink. She looked maybe ten years older than Oliver and didn't give any sign of realizing he existed, or that he stared after her longingly as she returned to her seat.

It was all very tragic. Finn made a mental note to avoid being the Oliver in that situation.

Vivi came through the door just after six thirty, in a pale pink sweater and form-fitting light blue jeans Finn planned to ignore so as to avoid what her mother would call Satan's impulses. Vivi radiated tension until she caught sight of Finn and relaxed. Maybe she'd worried Finn might stand her up.

As if.

Will came around the counter to give Vivi a hug. She hung onto him longer than Finn might have expected. When she let go and he pulled back, Finn recognized his expression with no trouble whatsoever. Finn wasn't the only one worried for Vivi.

Vivi led Finn to the furthest possible table from the counter, though. Will tried not to be obvious about watching them go, but his face kept the concern.

"I'm sorry," Vivi said once they were settled. She played with the paper from her straw as Finn adulterated her one allowable daily cup of non-medicinal coffee with cream, for a change of pace. "Thanks for showing up, especially the day after Christmas and after how I acted. I wanted to apologize, and not by text. I'm sorry, Finn. I'm glad you're out, and I'm glad we ran into each other. Can we start over?"

She looked up to meet Finn's eyes. Finn's heart caught at how small she seemed, tired and guilty. At least Finn could wipe out that last part. "Of course we can. Don't worry about it, you have a lot going on. I'm here if you need me. I've lost count of how many times you've saved me, you know?"

Vivi tried to smile, but her eyes filled up with tears and she covered her mouth. "I'm sorry," she said again, her voice breaking. "I'm crying about every little thing suddenly. Distract me? How was your Christmas?"

Finn glanced across the cafe to check on Will's whereabouts in case Vivi didn't want him to see her tears, but he was deep in a conversation with a customer, a thin, elegant person in a pretty dress and cardigan. He appeared to be reassuring them about something. Finn handed Vivi her napkin.

"My Christmas was fine." No way was Finn bringing up the housing bombshell. "None of the kids ate any wrapping paper bits as far as we know, so we called it a win. How was yours?"

Vivi blotted beneath her eyes to keep her mascara from running. "It was okay. Either my stepmom brokered a cease fire or Nora went over there behind my back and yelled at Dad ahead of time. But it was a *lot*, especially because I haven't told them, any of them, about this." She gestured to her midsection. "I got through all of Christmas Eve and Christmas Day with them and I didn't say a thing, can you believe it? It's just… this wasn't intentional. I have to make a decision pretty soon and honestly I don't know what to do."

Okay, that was a lot to deal with. Finn had been correct about the something's-wrong vibe.

"Yeah," Vivi said, her voice twisting. "I know what you're thinking. I'm a nurse, I know how these things happen, so how exactly did I screw up like this?"

And *that* was a lot of hurt. "I would never," Finn assured her. "It's nobody's business but yours. Is one of your friends giving you grief about this?"

Vivi sniffed. "No. I don't have many friends in Austin yet, and I'm not talking about it at work. The guy isn't being a jerk either, but he's kind of overwhelmed. He's not even from here, he's back at school now in Mexico City, studying physics. We Facetimed. He's, uh, twenty one."

Seven years younger than Vivi. Finn didn't want specifics, but she had to respect that game. "Nice."

Vivi almost laughed. "Yeah, but not my best decision."

"Hey." Finn waited until Vivi met her gaze. "Enough putting yourself down, okay?"

Whereupon she had to get Vivi a couple more napkins. She also dragged her chair around to between Vivi and the counter. One advantage of being tall for a woman was she made a halfway decent privacy screen.

"I have about six weeks left to decide," Vivi whispered, "before I'd be past the cutoff in Texas and I guess I'd have to fly somewhere. It should be plenty of time, but it's like there's this ticking clock and it's so loud I can't think. I want kids someday but it wasn't in my plans for, y'know, right now."

Finn had no idea what to say. She'd never been there. Putting her foot in her mouth was probably worse than silence, so she made a sympathetic noise in lieu of words.

"Can we talk about something else?" Vivi asked, still watery but sitting up and squaring her shoulders. "This has consumed my entire brain lately and honestly I'm sick of thinking about it. Tell me about how the rest of your time went. Did the new nurses seem aware that prisoners deserve basic human rights?"

Finn didn't bother trying to hide her grin. She'd missed Vivi's outbursts so dang much. "They were mostly okay. The migraine the other day kicked my butt way harder than anything after you left."

"Oh thank goodness," Vivi exhaled. "Is your P.O. reasonable? You can probably ask to switch if they're not. I'm sure there's a site somewhere with your legal rights."

Finn nodded, because the guy was fine, but something

occurred to her. "You never asked what I did to end up in there."

Vivi's smile quirked up. "Unless you hurt somebody besides yourself, it's nobody's business but yours." She got serious and raised one eyebrow. "Did you?"

"Only economically, and not even by much, I swear." Nobody had gone without because of what she'd done.

"So we're fine unless you're planning to do it again, in which case get up and walk on out of here because I *cannot* watch you go back there again. I mean it, Finn."

Finn held up her hands for peace. "Not happening. I learned a lot from all that."

"Like what?"

"I'm terrible at crime."

When Vivi dissolved into giggles, Finn gave herself a mental gold star. If Vivi was serious about being friends, and being Vivi's friend meant making her laugh with her whole self, Finn could accept that mission.

"You're ridiculous," Vivi finally gasped. "How did I forget how funny you are?"

Finn shrugged. "It was a long time ago." And it was the past, and this was the present. She had to keep things clear.

"Not so long." Vivi met Finn's eyes with an expression Finn found a touch too familiar, enough to wonder *what*—

Then it was gone, Vivi moving away slightly and going back to fiddling with a clean napkin.

"Anyway," she said, a bit quickly to Finn's ears, "You seem different now. Not just the hair—though it looks fantastic, by the way. You stand up straighter now, maybe? I knew it was hard on you in there but I didn't realize how much. I wish I could have done more. The prison industrial complex is such a nightmare, and I simply cannot understand how people making these decisions go to bed at night believing they're good people."

Finn didn't want Vivi worrying about her, even retroactively. "I did okay in there. I promise. I read a lot of books I wouldn't have under other circumstances, and some of them were almost enjoyable."

Vivi smirked. "You missed your real library card."

"And my Netflix account. But nobody messed with me too bad and now I'm moving forward."

Forward with finding some way not to end up living in Waco, and forward with putting her feelings for Vivi aside, mildly confusing too-long eye contact notwithstanding.

Vivi tapped her fingers on the side of her mug. The room had gotten darker. Will moved around the seating area, turning on small lights, including the ones inside the star-shaped paper lanterns hanging from the ceiling at pleasingly random intervals.

"So," Finn said once he'd moved back out of hearing range. "How's the clinic job?"

Even with Vivi's exhaustion, she perked up. "I love it. My stepmom wants me to go back to an E.R. to make more money, but I am not interested in that level of risk anymore. I felt safer at the prison. But it's inspiring to be on a care team again where everyone's on the patients' side, you know? If there's fighting, it's us together fighting the insurance companies or the underfunding of charity care. I feel so fortunate every day I go to work, especially because our workplace culture is accepting and I can be out. Aaand now I'm a human recruiting video, sorry."

Finn risked patting Vivi's hand, since that was a friend thing. She'd have done the same for Hollis. "Don't worry, you don't. Nursing being your jam is one of the things I've always admired about you." It sounded silly, but Finn truly enjoyed the way Vivi sparkled when she described an exciting continuing education course or a fascinating journal article she'd read. She was a nerd, and her nerdiness was all about helping people. What wasn't to like?

Vivi's smile softened, and Finn thought she could see a hint of wistfulness in it. "Thanks. You give the best compliments."

Finn would have been a liar if she said those words didn't make her heart soften like Vivi's smile, but that was hers to deal with, not Vivi's, so she would deal with it. Finn leaned away, and scooted her chair back to where it had been for good measure.

Vivi watched her do it, her expression changing to something unreadable.

When Finn was settled, however, Vivi gave her a solid not-gonna-cry-again smile, and they talked. Finn recounted the sketchiest job ads she'd seen so Vivi could strenuously denounce them. Vivi gave her vegetarian restaurant recommendations and Finn avoided mentioning she couldn't afford to eat out. She was skeptical of the Russian sushi place anyway.

Finn told Vivi about the latest on her parents, which wasn't anything new. Her mother was still in love with a twisted version of Jesus, and still writing Finn letters all about it; her dad was still trying to ignore the whole situation. Vivi tried to convince Finn that Nora would warm up with time. Finn opined she'd prefer to meet Alicia, because if it came to a fight, Finn figured she could take an actuary.

Vivi's eyes widened. "You remember Alicia takes Krav Maga, right?"

Well damn.

"Kidding! Oh wow, your face."

Finn chose not to respond. She had perfectly fine coffee that needed drinking.

When Vivi eventually said she had to go, Finn walked her to her car. One advantage of being related to the owner, it turned out, was parking in one of the spots behind the building marked Reserved For Staff.

"I know it makes no sense to come here to talk about stuff when I don't want them to know yet," Vivi explained as she dug her keys out of her purse, "but nothing in there smells wrong and right now that's a key factor."

She unlocked her light blue Honda Fit and turned back to Finn. "Thank you. I needed this. A friend, like you said. Friends are good, right?"

Finn put her hands in her jacket pockets to keep them warm. She hadn't been planning to mention the knocked-up thing again, since Vivi wanted a break from it. But if she was hesitating to tell other people, Finn couldn't let her leave without knowing somebody had her back.

"I'm on your side." She looked down at Vivi. "Whatever you decide is right for you. If you want me to put a crib together, or you want me to drive you to the clinic and back home, I'm there."

Vivi hadn't been lying about tearing up at everything. Her eyes got glisteny, and her chin began to wobble. "You really mean it, don't you?"

"Yeah, I really do."

Vivi swallowed. "Thanks. That means so much. And I wanted to say... I think about those two years a lot. Seeing you every day. I guess I didn't know if you did too. If you do, still?"

Finn did think about prison. It was hard to avoid, since her daily life now was such a stark contrast. Crossing a street, boarding a bus, buying a cup of coffee. Some of it was positive contrast, bursts of pleasure where for so long there had been grey. Except for Vivi, who'd always been full color. Lots and lots of pink, especially. Finn hadn't known she liked pink so much until Vivi showed up in her life.

It wasn't fair to Vivi for Finn to stay mired in all that, however, and it probably wasn't best for Finn's mental health either. She did her best to sound resolute and reassuring. "I'm putting it behind me."

Vivi stepped back. Finn hadn't realized they'd gotten so close. Vivi nodded roughly, got into her car, hastily waved through the window, and pulled out of the parking space.

Finn waited until Vivi's car had turned out of the parking lot. She walked over to the restaurant's back wall and leaned against it.

Dammit! A second chance, and she'd blown it somehow.

The New Year couldn't come soon enough. Maybe January would be Finn's clean slate. Maybe then she could finally get something right.

CHAPTER SEVEN

Someday, Finn would have secured an affordable place to live and also cleared her debts to both Hollis and the criminal justice system. Her next step would be throwing money at the Austin Public Library. Not only out of gratitude for the books and a warm place to hang out between ten a.m. and nine p.m., but for the free internet access.

Without it, she might not be staring at a response to all her job searching, one surprising enough to distract Finn from her enormously unsettled emotions.

A dentist's office from the queer chamber list had obviously gotten confused. *We received your inquiry and resume. We unexpectedly have a front desk and supply management position open with a January 2 start date. Below is the link to our online application. Please fill it out promptly.*

Not a lead to, like, a janitorial position. An invitation to apply in their own office. Finn clicked through to the application, expecting a screen with *Ha Ha Just Kidding* or a multilevel marketing scam for essential oils, maybe. But as far as she could tell, it was a real application for a real office job, doing receptionist stuff and restocking supplies, with paid time off and health insurance.

The application had the box. The one you had to check if you'd been convicted of a felony. If Finn came down with carpal tunnel, it would be from how many times she'd checked that box in the past few weeks. She cringed each time she saw it, not because she didn't want to check it, but because she hadn't thought twice about it in her old life as a hiring manager for the cashier team. Of course an employer would want to know if someone had gone to prison, right?

In her new life, she wondered how the ever-loving heck people without a Hollis were supposed to avoid lives of crime after serving time. If you couldn't get a legal job, how were you supposed to pay rent or buy a bus pass or replace your shoes when they fell apart? Non-disabled adults like Finn could get food stamps for a while, but they weren't generally eligible for cash welfare, at least in Texas.

This box had another box after it, for explanatory text. Finn considered making it formal the way she had in her cold emails: *I made a mistake I deeply regret, I've done my best to repay my debt to society, and I'm hoping to make a fresh start to be a contributing member of society.* Except she had a better version saved in the cloud, because she couldn't use "society" twice so close together.

She doubted it changed a single mind to read the same stock phrases every ex-offender pasted in to signal they'd either mended their ways or were savvy enough to pretend. She filled out the rest of the application, leaving the explanation field until the very end. When she couldn't put it off any longer, she took a deep breath. What the heck, why not tell the absolute truth?

I stole money from my employer and gave it to other staff. There's no excuse. I wish I'd never done it and if I were the judge, I'd have thrown the book at me too. So I went to prison and now I need a job.

Finn pressed Submit before the overthinking part of her brain got a second wind. She couldn't do worse applying for this job than she had on the other 56 jobs she'd applied for. Plus, it was low risk because she didn't have any real chance of getting this kind of job. Like how your odds of winning the lottery didn't improve, statistically, by buying a couple of tickets, because you could also find one on a park bench or something. Applying was just another entry in her job search log.

She left the library an hour later to get some sunshine. She turned on her phone's ringer so she didn't have to keep wondering if every random vibration in the universe could be a call about a job.

That was the only kind of call she expected after not hearing from Vivi in three days. Finn had no idea what to do with that, or if she was even supposed to do anything. If Hollis had been medically eligible to get a beer or three with Finn at a bar, she'd have unloaded the whole mess on him. Hollis, being older and wiser, would say, *Have you talked to her about it?*

Which was fair since texts and calls went both ways, but having made Vivi cry and run away in their last encounter, Finn had no idea what she'd say. Maybe Vivienne Curiel just wasn't meant to be part of her life anymore. She'd been there when Finn desperately needed her. She'd showed up again briefly to… what, exactly?

Maybe to inspire Finn to make a difference in the world. Perhaps fate had wanted to remind Finn how passionate Vivi was about nursing, and encourage Finn to find her own path. She definitely spent plenty of time these days reflecting on how some combination of mental health treatment, substance abuse treatment, protection from an abuser, or a job paying a living wage would have likely kept the vast majority of Finn's fellow prisoners from ending up there. Instead of helping them, society locked them up.

Maybe, once Finn could afford stable shelter, she was supposed to take a page from Vivi's book and do something about it.

She sat down to ponder that possibility and almost immediately got a text.

It was Vivi. Finn almost shook her head at the coincidence, except she'd been thinking about Vivi several times an hour for three days. No way for the gal to contact her without it seeming like fate.

Can I make you dinner tonight? Gonna be bland sorry in advance.

Vivi's definition of bland might be different than Finn's. From what Finn had heard, Vivi's Mexican-American stepmom had never seen a hot pepper she didn't want to be friends with. Finn had been raised on uninspired white-people cuisine featuring the contents of far too many cans. Prison food was quite similar, it had turned out, much to Finn's dismay.

Dismay. A perfect word for how Finn felt about the goodbye in the parking lot. Was it going to turn out any different if she said yes to another get-together? On the other hand, was Finn going to say no to Vivi?

I'll be there. What time?

The reply came back instantly. *7?*

See you then. Can I bring anything?

No thanks.

That gave Finn three hours before she'd need to rummage up a bus and head south. Before Finn could head back into the library, her phone rang. She didn't recognize the number, which meant she had to answer it, because her job search meant it could be anyone. Finn had hung up on more telemarketers in the last three weeks than she had in her whole prior life.

"Hello, this is Ellen Finnegan," she said, in what she hoped was a pleasant and professional tone.

"I'm calling from the dental office of Dr. Choi."

Finn had to stop herself from pulling the phone away from her ear to stare at it. She'd sent in the application as requested. Had it not gone through and they were calling to yell at her for not applying? You'd think nobody would have time for that kind of thing, but people could be strange.

"Ms. Finnegan, I know this is short notice, but would you be available for an interview at twelve thirty tomorrow? Our office is normally closed between Christmas and January 2nd but we need to fill this position as soon as possible."

An interview. For a real job, a salaried office job. Vivi's call might have been unexpected, but this was verging on absurdity.

Finn paused before responding. *Don't sound desperate or disbelieving. Use complete sentences.* "Yes, I can be there."

The caller made sure Finn knew exactly where the office was before hanging up, and then Finn located a chair on the library's little stone porch she could safely collapse into. Hollis had paid for her to buy an interview suit despite her protesting it was overkill. What kind of interview would she get that needed more than her khakis and a clean button-down?

She was going to bring that man cake every day for the rest of his life once she could afford it.

An interview didn't mean a job. A job didn't mean an apartment. But at the very least, Finn would get practice convincing a hiring manager that she was a newly upstanding citizen who had put even the most trivial of misdemeanors behind her.

Tonight, though, Finn had to get through dinner without accidentally stepping on Vivi's toes again. If she couldn't, Finn would just have to call it a loss and move on before she did any more damage.

CHAPTER EIGHT

Finn had to wait a minute or so before Vivi answered her knock on the apartment door. Vivi's hair was loose again, falling down around her shoulders like a river of darkness that melted into a field of flowers. She'd changed into comfortable clothes, pink swishy cotton pants which weren't quite pajamas, and a light grey t-shirt with tiny pink stars all over it. Her face was bare, which Finn had never seen before. It was a different kind of pretty, simpler and more vulnerable.

She appeared tired, but not falling apart, and either more peaceful or resolved to act like it. Either way, she didn't seem to have invited Finn over to yell at her under the pretext of dinner, so at least Finn was starting from zero instead of negative numbers.

Vivi went back to the stove as Finn followed her. "These are the least interesting quesadillas in history. I did warn you."

As long as Vivi could keep them down, no problem. Finn took off her jacket and parked herself on one of the two barstools at the kitchen counter. "Just don't try to serve me canned pears on the side and we're fine."

Vivi turned around with the pan in one hand, a spatula in the other, skepticism on her face. "Why would anyone put a pear in a can?"

"I promise they're even worse than they sound." Finn held up an empty plate so Vivi could slide a quesadilla onto it.

Vivi sat too, and polished off most of her food in the time it took Finn to eat a quarter of hers. Here Finn had thought applying the word *inhale* to food was a metaphor.

"Sorry," Vivi said, taking a break to sip her water. "I'm actually hungry for a change." She met Finn's eyes only for a moment before spearing another bite.

"I have no complaints. Thanks for the invite. Much better company than some of the places I eat these days."

Vivi stared at her.

"Oh," Finn said, realizing how she might have sounded. "I meant, I take a sandwich when I leave Hollis's in the morning, and usually I eat outside of the library or whatever. There's pigeons and squirrels and stuff. Not big talkers." She *had* ended up in a couple of, uh, educational conversations with a few humans while dining al fresco. She now knew more about cryptocurrency and kombucha than she ever had before.

Vivi's eyes filled with tears. Again. The constant waterworks had to be exhausting.

"Fuck," Vivi said. "I'm sorry, it's not you, it's me. Give me a minute." She got up from the kitchen island, wiping her eyes, and walked into the living room. As Finn watched, she dropped to the couch only to bury her face in her hands.

Did she need space? Comfort? Finn didn't have the first clue.

"I'm sorry," Vivi called from behind her hands. "This isn't what I meant to happen tonight. I'm a disaster."

"You're not a disaster! I'm clearly the one who owes an apology here so tell me what to apologize for. Or I can make something up. Lady's choice."

Whereupon Vivi burst into hard jagged sobs as if nothing would ever be okay again.

It was too much to watch, so Finn walked over to the couch and sat down. "Hey there. Hey."

Vivi just sobbed.

It was harder than Finn had anticipated to not to wrap an arm around Vivi, whisper comfort, call her sweetheart. If Vivi was crying this often, Finn would have to stay on guard, no matter how much she wanted Vivi to be leaning into somebody instead of trying to go it alone.

When the tears wound down, Finn realized it might well be her role in life to fetch paper products for pretty girls. She went to bring Vivi a box of tissues and the little aqua trash can from the bathroom. She busied herself clearing Vivi's dishes to give the poor woman time to blow her nose in privacy. When Finn settled back on the couch, she tried again.

"You're not a disaster," she repeated. "You have a big decision to make, and you don't feel like you can rely on your family for support. That's a rough place to be."

Vivi pushed her hair back, still looking miserable. "I'm being unreasonable. I know I am. I'm just tired of Nora and Allie trying to solve everything for me because I'm the youngest. I considered telling my stepmom, but if I keep it, she'll be so relieved because she'd want a grandkid so bad. I don't want to put that between us. You know?"

Finn made a noise of agreement.

"Nora and Will don't want kids," Vivi went on, obviously trying to pull herself together. "Matt wants kids, but it hasn't happened for them and Alicia's not motivated enough to do a bunch of tests or adopt. She talks about it with anybody, by the way, I'm not sharing without permission. Of course my dad would be relieved if I married the guy, which is very much not on the table."

That was a whole lot of information about everybody except the person who mattered. "Vee, what do *you* want?"

Vivi ducked her head as if she was ashamed. "I don't know if I want to be a single mom, but I don't know what they're going to think of me if I have an abortion, and my hair's a mess and my nails are chipped and everything is so confusing."

That wouldn't do. Finn tipped Vivi's chin up with her fingertips and met her eyes squarely. "Anyone who thinks less of you for getting health care can talk to me, and your hair looks wonderful and your nails are pretty. Okay?" Finn brushed aside a couple of escaping tears.

Vivi froze.

Finn pulled her hand back. "I'm so sorry. I didn't mean to—"

Vivi scrambled up and took a few steps away from the couch, her arms going around herself. "No, I'm sorry. I'm trying to respect your boundaries."

Finn's *what*?

"You've been clear," Vivi continued, her eyes still wet. "I know the situation we met in was fucked up, so it's okay, I understand. I was the only person who would give you your fucking medication on time, and maybe the only one who treated you like you mattered. I tried to, anyway. I promise I did know that maybe what I thought you were feeling was a reaction to the situation and not about me. Or maybe I was misreading you through wishful thinking because to be totally honest, I was really lonely working there and you were, like, the only other out queer person I saw on a regular basis."

Finn hoped her dizziness wasn't pre-migraine. At least

with her spray in her pocket, she might not go down in two days' worth of flames this time.

"So I'm sorry." Vivi took a half-step back, and her voice broke. "I'm screwing this up. I may need time to get my head together before we can be friends. I want to, I really do, and it hurts more than I expected it to but that's my problem, not yours. If I were a better person I wouldn't have said anything, but of course I can't ever keep my mouth shut."

Okay, what?

Maybe Finn was jumping to conclusions. It would be better if she was. She had nothing to offer Vivi, not right now, hence why she'd been trying so hard and committing herself to moving on. Finn had been… getting the entire picture backwards?

"I suspect we need to talk," Finn suggested weakly. She kinda wanted to kick herself. This might be a terrible idea. Who knew how long she'd even be living in Austin, at this rate?

"Do we have to? I can suck it up. Last time I'll say anything, cross my heart." Vivi did the little heart-crossing gesture. "Or if you need a break for me to get my act together and we can try again later, I get it. I don't want to put you in an awkward situation."

Vivi sounded so beaten down, Finn was tempted to let it go. But. In prison she'd wanted those five magical minutes, the chance to hear Vivi say how she felt, and to do the same herself. Maybe now was the time. Whatever the outcome, they could finally have that.

"I think we should," Finn said. "I'll go first as long as we both agree to tell the absolute truth. All of it."

It would be a first for them. Nobody else was listening. Nobody's job was at stake, no one's limited amount of freedom or medical care. Simply two women alone in a room finally being honest. From the way Vivi was staring at Finn, that liberty was hitting them both the same way, hard and sad and giddy all at the same time.

"Yes," Vivi agreed, though she sounded wary. "Okay."

Finn pulled one knee loosely up to her chest. Armor, if she was misreading the situation yet again and might get metaphorically kicked in the heart. She'd asked for honesty and she wasn't going to back out now, even if her hands would be shaking if she wasn't using them to hold her leg in place.

She looked up at Vivi, at her beautiful exhausted face and her guarded eyes. "I'm in love with you, Vivienne. That's been true for a long time."

Vivi's mouth dropped open, the same way it had when she'd recognized Finn in the hall at the clinic. When she closed it, an expression came over her face that Finn knew all too well.

Finn was about to get a lecture.

"Then why have you been doing this whole *let's be friends* thing? Do you know how much that hurt?" Vivi's eyes flashed and her hands went to her hips. "I missed you so much I cried for a *month* after I got fired! And you appear from out of nowhere and act like nothing ever happened?"

Technically nothing had, in the *violation of ethics and correctional policy* kind of way, but Finn knew what Vivi meant. Calling it nothing erased all their time working together, how they'd depended on each other, and their in-jokes nobody else understood. Gone would be Vivi's whispered confession she was also queer, trusting Finn not to tell anyone. The fond glances would disappear, and so would the longing ones, and that one brief instinctive touch. The touch Finn had alternately tried to block out and cherish during the months after Vivi had gone and Finn had been left behind and everything, everything, had seemed so very much more hopeless.

Apparently Vivi was only getting started. "I asked you why you were at the clinic and you held your paperwork up like how could I possibly assume you were there for me. As if I hadn't had a hundred daydreams of running into you? And you wanted to get *caught up*? Like oh, hey, we used to work together, so let's swap a few funny memories from the office and I'll show you pictures of my cat and we'll call it a day?"

Finn didn't remember any sign of a litterbox. "You have a cat?"

"I don't have a cat!" Vivi threw up her hands in frustration. "I'm allergic to cats!"

Finn was never telling Hollis about this. Not ever. He'd gone through surgery and so much physical therapy and he'd destroy all his progress by laughing at her so hard he re-injured himself. Finn might have laughed too if it were happening to someone else.

"I'm so sorry," she said desperately. "Vivi, I'm so sorry. I misunderstood what you wanted. I misunderstood literally everything. Would it help if I grovel? A lot?"

"I don't know!"

"Would it help if I tell you I'm a terrible person?"

"But it's not true!" Vivi yelled. "You're a wonderful person! You're patient and kind and level-headed and hard-working and responsible and I'm in love with you too!"

What a lot of adjectives to live up to.

Wait. That wasn't the important part. *Wow. Okay.* Finn hadn't made it up. They really had… fallen in love.

And it was still there after all this time.

"I tried so hard," Vivi said sadly. "I tried so hard not to pressure you. I never wanted you to feel like you owed me anything, or like you wouldn't get care at the clinic unless you said yes to something I asked. Allie told me to keep trying to leave you space to tell me."

Instead Finn had told Vivi they were friends, that she didn't have an agenda and the past was behind them. Finn had thought she was the worst butch ever for the migraine catastrophe, but this? This was next level. Vivi knew where Finn was in her life, what she was facing, and she'd kept holding the door open for Finn all the same. Even when Finn had charged off in the opposite direction.

"Vee, I'm so sorry. I've possibly set a world record here for number of signals missed." She'd wanted Vivi so much. Why hadn't she jumped at the hint of a chance? Thinking back now, some of the signs had been pretty dang clear. Finn just hadn't seen them properly. With Vivi under so much pressure, Finn couldn't add any more. "I wanted to be careful. With you."

Vivi's shoulders dropped, and she stared at Finn for a second, her expression changing. "Maybe with yourself too?" she asked gently.

Damn. That hit something, enough to keep Finn from from talking because of the lump in her throat. She'd lost so much when she went to prison, almost everything but Hollis. Maybe it had been safer not to ask for more.

She did want more, though, and by what felt like an impossible miracle, so did Vivi. Whatever lay underneath Finn's misreadings until now, she wasn't going to let it cause her to make the same mistake for a fifth or sixth time.

Finn wiped her sweaty hands on her jeans and got to her feet, wishing she'd worn a nicer shirt. She walked slowly towards Vivi, giving her plenty of time to move out of the way, plenty of time to give some indication she wanted space. She didn't. Finn paused anyway when she got close.

"Do you want this? Still?" Finn had never envisioned

adding *still* to the end of the question, but she hadn't expected so many wrong turns on her way to asking it. "I don't have a lot to offer right now. Except me."

"Yes," Vivi insisted, maybe a touch desperate for Finn to hear her. "I want this. Do you? I mean, if… I don't know what it would look like. If I don't have an abortion, I mean."

Finn had never dated somebody with a kid, but surely they could figure it out. Dates would probably involve a stroller, but that sounded just fine. "I'm pretty sure it would be me helping when you need help, and following your lead because it's your kid. Either way, whatever you choose, it doesn't change my feelings. I want you to be my girl."

She made sure not to hold her breath or lock her knees while she waited for a verdict. When Vivi beamed, bright and relieved, it was like the sun coming out. Finn wanted to kiss her, but the moment, the truth in it, felt too new and too fragile. All she could do, what felt right, was to pull Vivi in, press a kiss to her temple, and hold her.

It was more than everything she'd imagined it would be. Vivi was warm, curvy and squishy in so many lovely places. She snuggled herself into Finn's arms and made a half-pained half-relieved sound. Finn empathized. So much wasted time. So much abundance here and now.

She stroked Vivi's hair. "I'm sorry," she said again. "I never meant to hurt you."

"I missed you," Vivi said into Finn's shoulder. "I missed you so much. Nobody's ever gotten me the way you do. You *listen*. I mean, under normal circumstance."

Vivi had said Finn gave the best compliments. Finn might beg to disagree.

"I missed you too," Finn said. "No one else would get me coffee from the staff break room."

The gorgeous brunette in her arms made an outraged noise and poked Finn right in the ribs.

Finn faux-protested and twisted away, but Vivi got her again, and then they were both laughing, tangled up and turning and mostly not stepping on each other's feet, until Vivi stumbled and Finn caught her. They were *not* capping this ridiculous, wonderful evening with a trip to the emergency room, especially if Nora would find out, which of course she would.

"You good?" Finn wanted Vivi steady on her feet before she let go.

"Very," Vivi whispered.

Suddenly Finn was acutely aware that Vivi smelled exceptionally good, tart like citrus or cherries. "Hey." She couldn't remember any other words.

Vivi, fortunately, didn't have the same problem. "I really want to be kissing you right now."

So after months and months and what felt like years and years of wanting to kiss Vivienne Mary Curiel, Finn finally did.

It was perfect. Tender, sweet, and somehow they both knew where to put their noses, and neither of them forgot to breathe. Vivi leaned into Finn, dropped her hands to Finn's hips, and held on, making a small sweet humming sound and chasing Finn's mouth for more.

"Do you have to be anywhere right now?" Vivi asked when they paused. She was flushed and her hair was a bit mussed.

Finn almost laughed. Nothing short of a crowbar could get her out of this apartment before Vivi wanted her gone. "Flexible schedule, remember?"

"Yeah." Vivi sounded like she was waiting for it to sink in. "You can stay for a while. Here. In my apartment. This isn't a dream. And oh fuck, I never let you finish your dinner, I'm so sorry!"

Turned out quesadillas were fine out of the microwave. By the time they'd eaten and not looked at pictures of anyone's cat, Vivi had yawned twice.

"Do you have to go?" she asked again, but a little more serious this time.

Finn had already texted Hollis about being out late. She could send him another text redefining late.

"I don't need to be anywhere but here."

CHAPTER NINE

Finn sat on the edge of Vivi's bed waiting for the gal to brush her teeth. These sheets were silkier than the ones she'd put on the couch for Finn a few days ago, that sateen stuff, white with pink polka dots. Vivi was such a *girl*. Finn planned to enjoy the hell out of that for as long as Vivi let her.

Vivi came back out of the bathroom wearing white pajamas, a matching tank top and little shorts. Finn enjoyed the hell out of those too. She'd never seen Vivi's upper arms and bare shoulders before. As lovely as they were, they had nothing on those big beautiful thighs, which Finn probably should stop staring at. And she would. Any second now, she would look up at Vivi's face.

Only problem was, Vivi's tank top was between Point A and Point B, and Finn's longstanding policy of not staring at Vivi's amazing tits would be sorely tested given the lack of bra between them and Vivi's shirt at that particular moment. A moment Finn would not have predicted a few hours ago: Finn sitting on Vivi's bed, with everything between them new, different, and full of hope.

Finn finally managed to drag her eyes up to meet Vivi's.

“Do you want me to change?” Vivi offered, pulling down on the hem of her shorts. “I wouldn’t have worn it if I didn’t want you to look, but you seem a little uncomfortable.”

Finn swallowed, her throat suddenly gone dry. “I would not describe my current state as uncomfortable.”

Vivi raised an inquisitive eyebrow and Finn had to swallow again. Did the woman have even the first clue how sexy she was? *There* was a word Finn had never been allowed to think near Vivi before. Sexy. Hot. Touchable.

Close.

“It’s okay if you’re not ready for anything physical,” Vivi said. “We can just sleep, if you’re tired.”

Though Finn appreciated how she didn’t hear the slightest hint of pressure in Vivi’s voice, sleep was the last option she’d choose right now. “After seeing you in that outfit, I may never be tired again.”

That got Finn a slow, mischievous smile. Vivi stepped closer until her legs bumped against Finn’s knees. Taking a deep breath, Finn eased her legs apart slowly until there was enough room for Vivi to get one of hers between them. Vivi straddled her, surrounding Finn’s thigh in pillowy warmth.

“I’m really, really glad you’re here,” Vivi said, low and quiet.

Finn stopped to take a breath. Leaned forward until her forehead rested on Vivi’s chest. Vivi’s hand came up to Finn’s hair, pushed the top part over to one side, smoothed down her undercut. “Do you keep this up yourself?”

“Hollis does it.” Finn licked her lips, feeling Vivi’s body heat, acutely aware of the close proximity of her breasts and the lush, rich curves of her belly and hips.

“I like it.” She smoothed the short hair again before letting her fingertips trail down the back of Finn’s neck. “I like *you*.”

Do something, Finn. She's right here!

Finn brought her hands up to Vivi's legs, finding smooth skin and squeezable softness. Hearing a little satisfied sigh, Finn moved her hands a little higher and did it again, doing her damn best to respect the hemline of Vivi's shorts even though there was so much more of Vivi's skin and Finn desperately wanted to touch that too.

She pressed a kiss to Vivi's sternum, then another beside it. Vivi stroked Finn's hair back again, trailed her fingers down Finn's cheek. Vivi's touch gave Finn the courage to find the curve of Vivi's breast with her lips, start mapping it out, nuzzling into her. Vivi's inhale made everything between Finn's navel and knees even more electric.

Moving her hips forward got Vivi up against the hot pressure between Finn's legs. Vivi leaned into her with another of those sexy sharp breaths. Finn was remembering how this worked now, the pattern of actions and reactions, the ratcheting up of tension and desire and heart rates. Both of Vivi's hands were on the back of Finn's head now, drawing her in, and Vivi's breath stuttered as Finn ran her open lips across Vivi's nipple. When Finn did it again the other direction Vivi moaned and rocked against Finn, so Finn's right hand slid up over the little shorts, the tank top. She lifted the generous handful of Vivi's breast and squeezed.

Vivi *flinched.*

Finn yanked her hand back, heart just about jumping into her throat. Vivi put her hands up, appeasing. "I'm so sorry! Totally my fault. I should have warned you they're sore. Hormones."

Ah. Finn hadn't spent much time around pregnant people. She rested her hands on her own thighs where they couldn't do any more damage and did her best to look up at Vivi.

"You're really nervous," Vivi said softly, concerned.

It took a second for Finn to realize she was rubbing her palms against her thighs. She stopped. She'd been trying to dodge her skittishness, but Vivi wasn't wrong. It wasn't the pregnancy; it was more global. "Yeah. It's been a long time." Was that the reason, though? Probably not, if Finn was honest. "And I've never been with *you*."

Vivi's breath caught. She reached out to cradle Finn's cheek in her hand. It seemed as if she might say something, but she simply shook her head and took a small step back. Finn didn't know if she was supposed to stay or follow. In the end, she didn't have to ask, because Vivi leaned down and kissed her.

Their second kiss started as sweet as the first, but Finn tried to put everything into it, her desire, her gratitude, how hard she was going to work so Vivi never regretted choosing her. She hadn't imagined she could want Vivi more, but Vivi's deep kisses showed her otherwise, made Finn's whole body come alight. Vivi reached for Finn's hands, still kissing her, still connected, and brought them back up to her breasts.

"Let me help you," she whispered against Finn's lips.

All Finn could do was nod, breathless, feeling Vivi's hands cupped over hers and all that weight and softness. She didn't find words again until she'd stroked Vivi's nipples through her shirt, mouthed them through the thin cotton, then stood to help Vivi push the little white tank top up and over her head.

"You're so gorgeous," Finn blurted, because it was true. Vivi's breasts eased down even more without the shirt, beautiful tear shapes with large dark nipples. Her belly curved out above her waistband, rich and inviting. Her face and throat were flushed, framed by dark hair tumbling every which way, and her deep, intense eyes were everything Finn had ever wanted to see.

Vivi grinned. "When I saw you in the hallway at the clinic, looking like that, even in the split second before I knew it was you…"

Finn took Vivi's hand and pulled her to the bed and down onto it, Vivi laughing all the way until she was on her back and coaxing Finn on top of her.

Then Finn's entire world was Vivi's smooth skin under her hands and Vivi's sweetness in her mouth. She'd never felt anything better than the almost-ache of her own arousal and this beautiful, magical, passionate woman beneath her. Vivi was soft in ways Finn had barely dared to dream about, and her hands skimmed down Finn's ribs like a beautiful shiver while Finn kissed her throat, behind her ear, her collarbone.

Vivi ran one of her fingertips lightly over her own nipple and just *seeing* it was so damn sexy Finn wondered if she might die. Happily. No regrets.

"Put your mouth here again?"

Fuck dying. Finn laid an open-mouth kiss on Vivi's finger. She changed her angle for the next kiss, used her tongue, kept Vivi's hand there when she tried to pull it back.

"Keep going," Finn whispered, hoping it sounded sexy instead of bossy. From the breathless moan it provoked, she guessed Vivi appreciated it just fine.

She licked over Vivi's nipple as Vivi played with it, nipping and sucking at her finger too until both were slick and wet. Vivi was grinding up against Finn's stomach now, needy, making noises Finn would have swallowed up with kisses if her mouth hadn't been otherwise occupied.

She got a finger hooked into Vivi's waistband, tried to get her little shorts off, but they got stuck on those beautiful wide hips. Vivi wriggled, trying to help, and dissolved into giggles when their combined efforts utterly failed to coordinate. She stopped helping when Finn stripped off her own t-shirt, though, her mouth falling open as she watched. Finn wasn't going to slow down now, but she sure didn't mind the validation. The grey sports bra and blue boxer briefs went next, and finally Finn was naked with Vivienne Curiel and it was possibly the best decision she'd ever made.

She'd imagined making this last. But now she was here between Vivi's legs, staring down at her lust-struck face and the luscious curves and swells of her body, and the only thing Finn wanted in the world was to make Vivi come.

"I don't want to go too fast," she confessed, reaching to stroke Vivi's cheek.

Finn's hand was intercepted and Vivi curved it around her hip. "We can go slow next time."

Next time. They were going to have a next time. It was almost too much joy to hold.

When Finn went in for another kiss, Vivi caught Finn's lip and dragged it between her teeth, a sharp shock of pleasure. Finn hadn't known she'd like that sting. Vivi kissed her again, coaxed Finn's hand towards her pussy, but Finn kept getting distracted by Vivi's rolling hip and soft belly and inner thigh.

"Finn," Vivi pleaded.

"What do you want me to do?" Specific direction. That's what she needed.

"Fuck me? Two fingers? I've had so many dirty thoughts about your *hands*."

Finn had to drop her forehead to Vivi's shoulder for a second to breathe. "Yeah. That— Yeah."

Her first time feeling Vivi's pussy made Finn actually whimper, and she couldn't even feel embarrassed, because fuck's *sake* it was amazing. Satiny and slick and so, so hot. Her fingers wanted to map everything between Vivi's legs, stroking, luxuriating. She teased along the sides of Vivi's clit with her middle finger, pressed harder, started a slow circle. Vivi's moan of pleasure almost blew a fuse in Finn's brain.

It wasn't what Vivi had asked for, though, and Finn could do more of that later. They had time. Finally, after all the longing, all the waiting, all of the trying to push these emotions away, they had time. She straddled Vivi's thigh, her own cunt meeting skin, and slipped two fingers inside the woman she loved. She got her thumb in the right place to work Vivi's clit and let the motion of her own hips rock her hand. Vivi pushed up, taking her in, wrapping one arm around Finn's neck and the other around her back to pull them as close as they'd ever been.

"I missed you so much," Vivi gasped. "I love you, I love you."

Finn whispered the same things back, again and again, until Vivi arched up against her, tightening around her hand and shuddering with a loud cry. She caught Finn's lips in another bruising kiss, encouraging Finn to ride her thigh until Finn buried her face in Vivi's hair and dug her toes into the mattress as the pleasure exploded through her cunt and belly and heart.

After their heart rates had dropped, they both fought having to disentangle, even with all the stickiness and sweat. Finn's lip throbbed, which she did not mind at all, but Vivi fussed after they'd cleaned up and brought her a piece of ice wrapped in a damp washcloth. Which was probably smart since she had an interview tomorrow.

"I dig your wild side," Finn told her around the cloth. "Bite me whenever you want."

Vivi just laughed and told her to lie down.

Finn did. For the first time since she'd walked into the holding cell the day of her arrest, she was in a real bed with nice sheets, and the only lock on the door worked from the inside. A few minutes later, Vivi's fingers interlaced with hers. Finn squeezed them.

Vivi squeezed back. "Say it again?"

It took Finn a second to realize what she meant. "I'm in love with you, Vivienne Mary Curiel. I started falling in love with you the first time you put an ice pack on the back of my neck and I never, ever stopped."

"Will you tell me every day?"

Finn nodded. "You might want to set a ceiling on the number of times. Safety first."

Vivi rolled her eyes to the ceiling, but she was grinning, like *this person is ridiculous and I adore her*.

Finn could totally live with that.

Vivi seemed to have lucked out with quiet neighbors. Maybe they'd all get home at two in the morning and start using their table saws while tuning their motorcycle engines. For now, though, it was peaceful. Nobody rustling or thrashing in nearby bunk beds. Nobody crying at night hoping nobody else would hear.

It was the easiest Finn had fallen asleep in years.

CHAPTER TEN

Finn woke up to the sound of Vivi already up and doing something in the kitchen. She reached out and managed to pull her phone to her face. Well, that explained why Finn hadn't woken up early enough to assist. It was 5:37 in the morning.

She had an interview today. Since she wasn't gonna get the job, it wouldn't help with her ticking clock on staying in Austin, but knowing she had less than seven hours left before she had to be shaking someone's hand for an interview unsettled her stomach anyway.

First things first. Get up. Help Vivi. Finn collected her sports bra, shirt and briefs, wished she didn't have to pull dirty clothes back on, but got over it. She washed her face with one of Vivi's fruity soaps and used the spare green toothbrush from her migraine visit. Finn hadn't been able to keep from smiling when she'd seen it still sitting on Vivi's sink. Finn owned a toothbrush, obviously, but she liked this one better.

Vivi stood at the stove, stirring a pot of something that smelled like oatmeal. She glanced up when Finn walked in.

"What can I do?" Finn asked.

Vivi just smiled. She smiled for so long, Finn wondered if she had toothpaste on her face, but she also couldn't help but grin back. She was in Vivi's apartment. Vivi wore nothing but a silky-looking robe that was only loosely closed in the front. Finn approved of this entire situation.

"Sorry I woke you," Vivi said. "This is done, do you want some? My grandma always made it on the stove. Allie's been threatening to do a blind taste test on me but I swear it's different than when you make it in the microwave."

Finn made a mental note to learn how to make oatmeal on the stove. First she had to get a stove. "Sounds good. Thanks. You should have gotten me up."

Vivi shrugged and gestured at the cabinet door behind her. "Get the bowls? You need a regular sleep schedule for your migraines."

Finn got the bowls, and it took her only two guesses to find spoons thanks to the kitchen being so small. She took a barstool and perched on it, wondering whether she should bring up her interview. No, she decided. Disappointing Vivi again so soon when it didn't pan out might be more than Finn could handle, and she didn't want Vivi feeling like she had to fix any of Finn's problems.

Vivi spooned oatmeal into the two bowls. She pushed a small blue ceramic pot over to Finn. Brown sugar. "How is your head, by the way?"

Finn felt herself pull back a tiny bit while she took a few bites of the oatmeal. It wouldn't be the first time someone had second thoughts about how much management her migraines needed. Dark rooms, noise-canceling headphones, avoiding certain foods, and oh, the endearing pharmaceutical copays. Finn generally did ninety-nine percent of the management herself, but she'd failed spectacularly the other day.

Maybe now the giddy confession stage was over, Vivi was contemplating the future and didn't care for what she saw.

"You're okay with all this, right?" Finn asked, pointing to her head. She didn't know if she wanted to hear the answer. This had been going so well for, like, ten whole hours.

Vivi cocked her head, spoon halfway to her mouth. "What? Of course. Why wouldn't I be?" Before Finn could answer, Vivi's eyes narrowed. "Has someone else *not* been okay with it? Do I need to pay them a visit? Because I will educate the holy hell out of them until they're begging for mercy."

How could Finn not adore this woman? Which could be a problem if Vivi was backing off. "It was a long time ago. I'm over it, I promise."

Vivi shook her head slowly in disgust. "That is ridiculous. It's a *health condition*. You're not doing it to make other people's lives difficult. I only asked because this last one was so bad."

"So long as you're sure." Finn needed to hear it one more time. "If we're going to be—"

"Living together," Vivi supplied.

Finn dropped her spoon and had to catch it as it skittered along the top of the island. "Sorry. Say again?" Surely she hadn't heard right.

Vivi's face fell. "Oh. I assumed… We've wasted so much time, and if you move in, you wouldn't have to sleep on a couch."

In this situation, there was only one thing to do. Finn got off the barstool, walked around the island, and tilted Vivi's chin up gently. Then she bent down and kissed her. Brown sugar and warmth. Perfect.

Now for the harder part: saying no. This wasn't her

Austin solution. Finn couldn't use Vivi or put that kind of pressure on their relationship. If Ilsa was going to kick her out, Finn would cross that bridge when it happened.

"The idea sounds amazing," Finn said, trying to sound approving, not cold or commitment-shy. She stroked Vivi's cheek as a reassurance. "And as a lesbian, I am no stranger to the U-Haul phenomenon, but Vee, I can't pay rent or bills or even for my own food."

Finn knew Vivi was gearing up to argue before she opened her mouth. It was in the shoulders. "I'm already paying the rent! And you barely eat anything! I ate lunch with you five days a week for two years and you never cleaned your plate!"

"That was prison food. There was a reason I warned you to keep bringing your lunch instead of having them bring one up for you, sweetheart."

Finn hadn't intended the endearment as a distraction, but it worked. Vivi ducked her head like she was trying to keep a little special joy to herself. Finn slipped her arms around Vivi and let Vivi snuggle into her.

"All I'm saying is," Finn continued, "let me have some pride here. Plus, you've got a decision to make, not a lot of time left to make it, and one option might impact your space needs as well as your expenses." She hoped she hadn't come across as telling Vivi her business.

Vivi took in a long, slow breath, and pushed it back out as if it was a lot of work. She stepped back from Finn. "Yeah. Okay. We should probably eat."

The air didn't have the happy expectation tingle it had when Finn had walked in. She tried not to be obvious about watching whether Vivi was eating her food or just pushing it around.

Vivi eventually put her spoon down and rested on her elbows. “I have a lot of plans for the next few years. I did legislative advocacy with the Texas Nurses Association last session, and hell yes I want to be down at the Capitol again giving those people a reality check. I also want to get qualified to train other nurses in competent care for LGBTQIA-plus patients. I’m not sure I want to put any of that on hold or slow it down to raise a child. Not yet. Which sounds selfish, but I love my work.”

“Having an abortion isn’t selfish. Who are you afraid is going to judge you?”

Vivi smiled bitterly. “The dominant culture?”

Going out to kick a bunch of politically active conservative evangelical Christians in the shins at this early hour wasn’t practical, and wouldn’t fix anything anyway. Probably.

“I know it’s not *everyone*.” Vivi leaned more heavily on the counter. “Trust me, I’ve seen the opinion polling. But it feels like it, and now you’re here, but I don’t have time to get used to this before I have to decide, and I know I shouldn’t... Dammit. Are we still doing total honesty?”

Finn nodded.

“I don’t want to expect anything from you. About us. Even though part of me feels maybe like this is, I don’t know, a gift? Or a sign. You showing up now instead of a month from now. Fuck, I’m sorry, that’s way too much to put on you.” She looked away, biting her lip.

Finn didn’t have money. She didn’t have stability. She had a criminal record and debts, and her head sometimes threw the most amazing tantrums for no reason. She had love, though, and the ability to work her ass off. Maybe it could be enough.

“Whatever call you make,” Finn said, “I’ve got your

back. If that means pitching in with baby care, fine. If you're not ready to raise a kid yet, make the appointment and anybody who gives you flak about it can come talk to me. If you even want to tell anybody. Or if you do want to raise a kid, and you and I are together…"

Vivi made an *I'm listening* noise.

This was the kind of thinking about the future Finn would probably have preferred to keep inside, given her housing predicament, but it had nagged at her a bit last night in the dark. "I'd be interested in the situation with the other biological parent. I mean, I'm assuming it's not somebody who would object to… two moms? If it works out." Technically Finn thought she'd be a better dad type than a mom, but if she needed to gear up for bigotry, she'd better start now.

"He wouldn't have a problem with it. I met him at this queer party Will took me to."

Huh. Interesting. At lesbian parties she'd been to in her old life, Finn had been able to assume all the gals there were gal-inclined. Vivi would have gone to a queer party knowing at least some of the guys might be bi or pan, but not which ones. "How did you know he was…" She didn't quite know how to phrase it. Orientationally compatible?

"He wore a Bi Pride flag as a dress."

Fair enough. "What's his name?"

"Vicente."

A snicker got out. "Sorry, sorry, but Vivienne and Vicente is pretty adorable. Mexico's pretty great, are you sure you don't want to move there and see if y'all have something?"

"I like it *here*. And hey, shouldn't you be at least a bit jealous talking about him?"

Finn winked. "I've never been much for jealousy. Anyway, you were in my bed last night, not his."

Vivi grinned back, sly and satisfied. “More accurately, you were in mine.”

Also fair enough. Finn conceded the point with a satisfied nod and went back to her oatmeal.

CHAPTER ELEVEN

Finn frowned suspiciously at the iron. She'd set it for cotton. Her dress shirt was cotton. The shirt was still wrinkled.

"What's wrong?" Hollis asked from where he sat on the couch with his e-reader.

"Nothing!" She would not be defeated by this hunk of metal and plastic.

Hollis scoffed and got up. He was moving better this morning. "Did you get the green spray bottle?"

"No, I used the sprayer built into the iron like normal people do."

"Austin water is hard. The iron clogs up and not enough comes out. Go get it."

Finn went back to the laundry room. The kids had all decamped to the park with their mom, each wearing several layers, which had required a twenty-five minute process of applying and sometimes reapplying said layers until all three children were fully dressed at the same time.

Finn was grateful for their absence. She hadn't been excited by the prospect of answering seventeen thousand questions, not while she got ready. She didn't *know* why (a) the sky was blue or (b) spiders didn't grow to the size of people and eat everyone and start living in their houses, and she refused to research that second one right now.

By the time she got back, Hollis had the shirt draped differently, the corner of the ironing board poking into the top of the sleeve and other parts of the shirt folded all weird. *Show-off.*

"Let me do it," she protested, but he waved her off. He wet the shirt with broad, precise strokes and brought the iron down again. It hissed, and Finn hoped Hollis knew what he was doing. It did seem unlikely he'd buy her a shirt and then scorch it. Although she did put his favorite set of D&D dice in the blender with half a cup of orange juice when she was eight years old and he was twelve. He could conceivably be playing a long game.

"You were out again last night," he observed. "Everything okay?"

Finn felt slightly useless watching him work. "I texted you." For reasons which she was trying not to think about so she didn't blush. Blushing was the opposite of cool, composed, and mentally rehearsing answers to the twenty most commonly asked questions in interviews.

Hollis's mouth quirked up. "You didn't say from where."

Back to this again? Honestly, Finn could tell him at this point, but it felt kind of nice to have something private for once. "Things are looking favorable in that department," she allowed.

Hollis repositioned the shirt. It was considerably less wrinkled already and Finn didn't see any burn marks. "You want Great-Aunt Geraldine's ring? It's just sitting around in my dresser."

If he wasn't recently injured and also holding a hot piece of metal, Finn would have shoved him. "Enough, boyo. I may be a lesbian but I do know how to date someone without—"

Hollis cut her off with a peal of laughter at getting her good. He shook so hard with it he had to put the iron down. Finn stood there and listened, her heart melting or blooming or possibly visibly glowing in her chest. She hadn't heard him laugh since his accident. Not this laugh, not any other all-out laugh. She'd missed it so damn much.

When Hollis had entertained himself sufficiently with his own wit, he picked up the iron again and went to work on the shirt's back. "I'd never heard you sound the way you did in those letters. The ring's there if you need it, however; not like I'll be using it anytime this decade. And don't worry about me and Ilsa if you want to move on, we'll manage."

Finn wasn't entirely sure that was true. The number of kid-generated messes per square foot here was formidable, and Hollis wasn't back to driving. Yet Ilsa might want privacy and to find a new normal more than she wanted the housekeeping.

"I won't overstay my welcome," Finn promised.

Hollis picked up the iron and eyed her suspiciously. "Did Ilsa say something?"

"No," Finn replied honestly.

"Mom?"

Finn's lying face didn't work.

"Dammit," Hollis hissed, going back to the ironing, a little more forcefully now. "I told her not to mention it. We were just brainstorming."

Finn's breath caught. It was true. "When does Ilsa want me out by? I'll make it happen." Waco to Austin and back wasn't usually so bad on the highway unless there was construction. There was probably a bus. She could keep interviewing in town.

"Ilsa hasn't been the only adult in her own house since I got out of the rehabilitation place," Hollis said with a sigh. "She's terrified about keeping up with everything once she's alone, but also desperate for privacy to start dealing with her new reality. Honestly I think she'd pick you over me since you're completely self-sufficient and can do more chores. I have friends I could stay with here in town, though, who won't try to drive the devil out of me."

Finn had nowhere else. Her circle of friends in Fort Worth had been falling apart before she got arrested anyway, with people moving away and breaking up and whatnot. Then she'd been gone for years. Ilsa must know, and she felt trapped into letting Finn stay.

"This sucks." Finn had no right to complain, but it had popped out.

"Well," Hollis replied, "Let's hope this job interview is a step forward."

Which wasn't a reassurance Finn wouldn't be asked to leave. However, a practice interview *was* a step forward and she had to think about it as such. Practice meant she'd be ready when a more likely job opportunity came up. Something in mopping, perhaps, or pushing loads of laundry from place to place, as she now had experience with both.

Hollis finished her shirt and handed it to her carefully. "You picked dark blue because your lucky rainbow sports bra won't show through, didn't you?"

"Abso-freakin'-lutely." And it looked fantastic with the grey suit, thank you very much.

Hollis laughed again. Finn wondered if she could record it as a ringtone. "Go get dressed. Take a rideshare on my account, okay? Otherwise you'll get all sweaty on the bus and ruin all my hard work."

Finn went to protest, but Hollis cut her off.

"Listen up," he said. "You're one of my favorite people in the entire world and I am buying you a rideshare to your interview so you can get the job and buy your girlfriend something nice. Now scoot."

When Finn looked in the mirror as she was buttoning up her shirt over the lucky rainbow sports bra, her face seemed a bit pink. *Girlfriend.* A word she'd need to get used to again. Well worth it.

Now if only she could arrange things so she had to get used to a paycheck too.

CHAPTER TWELVE

Dr. Choi was unreasonably attractive. Even Finn could tell, and her libido had never so much as twitched in the direction of a dude. He had movie star cheekbones, hair that was either blessed by the gods or that he spent an hour styling each morning, and posture debutantes would kill for.

Finn was super glad Hollis had taken over ironing her shirt. Finn had to do something fantastic for the guy, even aside from paying him back and the daily cake thing. Maybe she'd buy him some dice.

"Dae-hyun Choi," he said as he shook her hand in the waiting room of his dental practice. "Dustin is fine."

She was not calling him by his first name, no sir. "Ellen Finnegan. Thanks for this opportunity."

"You go by Finn, right?" Dr. Choi motioned for her to follow him down a hall. They ended up in his office.

"Uh, yes. I'm a blond white lesbian named Ellen, so..." Was she supposed to have said she was gay? He couldn't ask, but she could volunteer it, right?

"Everyone thinks they're the first person to make an Ellen

joke." Dr. Choi nodded briskly. "Got it. Please, sit. Water? Coffee?"

"No thank you." She didn't want to end up wearing a beverage.

"Here's the deal," he said as Finn took the seat on the other side of his desk. "We hired someone, but her spouse got a job in Taiwan. We usually hire known quantities so we get a fit with our workplace culture, but we went through our personal networks and didn't come up with anybody who can start right away."

While Finn struggled to figure out if she was supposed to respond, Dr. Choi took a picture frame off his desk and turned it around. It was a wedding photo, his, with a gorgeous tall Black man, both of them exuberant in dove grey tuxes. Dr. Choi was a totally different person when he smiled. An approachable person.

"I'll explain it this way," he said. "I'm a bisexual Korean dentist, second generation immigrant on one side and third on the other. I'm married to a gay Black man who's a bus driver. That doesn't mean I know everything, but it does give me a low tolerance for ignorant garbage.

"So, for example, if you think disabled people just need to do yoga, or singular they isn't correct grammar, or it's funny when people speak English with with something other than a mainstream U.S. accent, this is not the place for you. Eventually your real attitude will slip out. Then you won't have a job anymore and I'll have to start over with hiring and training which is a real pain in the ass. If that's how it's going to go, you can save us both some hassle by leaving right now and I can get home to the lunch my husband's making."

Dr. Choi folded his hands on his desk and waited. Finn's mind raced. This was her first job interview in a long time, but she didn't remember anything like this.

Being truthful on the application hadn't disqualified her from getting an interview, so maybe she should keep at it? "I'm sure there's plenty I don't know, but if I mess something up and hurt somebody I'd want to know so I can stop." That was true; was the truth good enough?

"Then tell me about stealing from your employer."

She'd known this topic would come up, but had hoped for a couple of easy questions first. Hollis had helped her practice a professional answer, similar to the copy-and-paste answer she'd used for The Box before the application for this job. The copy-and-paste interview answer said there wasn't any excuse, which there wasn't, but there had been a reason. Maybe Dr. Choi would get the distinction.

"The first thing you should know," Finn said, aware she'd waited a beat too long, "is that if I had a time machine, I'd go back and whack myself on the back of the head the first time I even considered it."

She thought Dr. Choi's lip twitched, but his demeanor didn't change. "We'll take it as a given for this interview that you know you should act remorseful. Go on."

Not encouraging. "Okay. So. It was a family-owned nursery, and they also ran a landscaping business from the same location. I'd worked myself up to head cashier at the nursery and I was about to get promoted to assistant manager. However, the family's oldest son had been fired from three other jobs in a year. In he comes as manager, and the existing manager gets bumped down to assistant. From day one, we can all tell this guy is a problem. A lot of the people working for him are women, Latinx, or both. He doesn't have much good to say about either of those groups, and he says it loudly on a regular basis. With Human Resources being his aunt, nobody was going to do anything."

Dr. Choi nodded. "Human Resources usually exists to

protect the company anyway. But what about losing that promotion? Must have stung."

Finn couldn't deny it. Going from hourly to salaried would have meant sick days instead of either working through as much of a migraine as she could when her meds didn't cut it, or losing a shift.

"It did suck, yes." Were you supposed to say *suck* in an interview? "And yeah, when your new boss is terrible, you should go find another job. It takes time, though, and meanwhile this guy kept running his mouth, and some employees who agreed with him decided it was cool to run their mouths as if they were on Fox News or whatever, and he took over the scheduling so they got more shifts.

"A few of us went out for a drink. One of my coworkers said she'd figured out how to skim money from the POS system and we could redistribute it to staff who were getting screwed. I let myself get talked into it because I was tipsy and angry, which is a terrible way to make a decision about anything."

"Ah," Dr. Choi said.

She'd probably said too much. Dr. Choi was a fellow queer, but he was also a potential employer. *Practice interview 1, Finn 0.* Good to get all the mistakes out early. Right?

"Well," Dr. Choi said, relaxing back in his office chair and starting to appear a little more mortal, "why don't you tell me why you'd make a great addition to the team here?"

Finn's ears were broken. This guy had a husband at home cooking. Why waste his time to keep going as a formality? "Beg your pardon?"

Dr. Choi smiled, and yep, he did look different. The kind of guy you might grab a beer with if Finn hadn't sworn off drinking with colleagues ever again.

"Your former employers give a lot of money to local charities," he said, "and they're accredited by the Better Business Bureau. That's true. But it's interesting how tracking down a few former employees through their Yelp reviews can give a more complex perspective."

Finn could swear his eyes were actually twinkling.

Unfortunately for her, that was the high point of the interview. As she recalled it afterwards on the bus, she'd stumbled through explaining she worked best in a team environment, and her biggest strength was precision, and her biggest weakness was putting in more work than she was getting paid for, except she made it sound a tiny bit less ass-kissing, but not by much. Interview practice with Hollis hadn't been enough.

Dr. Choi hadn't asked any follow-up questions about her crime, probably to spare her the embarrassment, but he'd laid out the duties of the position. Inventory and restocking was easy. Taking calls to set appointments from a big New Year's marketing mailing she could figure out. Processing insurance claims was totally unfamiliar.

"We probably wouldn't have someone in your situation handling payments for at least the first six months. I'm sure you can understand."

That was when she'd known she wouldn't be getting this job, same as she couldn't get a retail job. No one wanted her hands near a cash register, electronic or otherwise. The dreaded *We'll be in touch* at the end, during the handshake, sealed it.

Finn didn't have time to stop at Ilsa's and change into casual clothes before meeting Vivi at Knockdown as they'd agreed. Vivi would see the suit, and Finn would have to admit why she was wearing it—without anything to show for it, unless proof of effort counted for something.

Since it was all she had, it would have to do.

CHAPTER THIRTEEN

"Nice suit." Nora looked as if giving the compliment made her mildly uneasy.

Finn took the decaf Nora handed her across the counter. From anyone else, Finn would have simply ignored the attitude, but this was Vivi's sister. If things worked out the way Finn hoped, she'd be seeing Nora regularly here at Knockdown and on major holidays at minimum. Finn would tolerate Nora's disapproval to be with Vivi, but it was going to be a long however-long if they didn't get this sorted out.

Finn also remembered, facing Nora's flat expression, that the woman had only been twelve when she'd lost her mom. She'd had to start raising her sisters, seven and nine, because their dad checked out for several years. It was possible Nora could use a bit of grace.

Also, for Finn to maybe stop assuming the worst about her. Vivi had said Nora would warm up and Finn needed to give her the opportunity. So Finn used her kindest voice. "I hope I get a chance to change your mind about me."

Nora put both hands on the countertop and leaned

forward. Her arm muscles made Finn's arm muscles more than a touch envious. "She cried about you."

Here Finn had assumed it was the ex-con thing.

"And," Nora added, "You just got out of prison."

Ah. It was also the ex-con thing.

"It's a hard road, starting over again," Nora went on. "Vivi has student loans. She wouldn't let me find a reliable used car, so she has a payment. I don't want her dragged down."

Fair. Finn had similar concerns herself. "These are job interview clothes. I am trying. I swear I will never, ever mess up Vivi being able to pay her bills. If I do, you can put me on the first bus out of town."

Nora sniffed, but it seemed more like surprise than disapproval. She stared at Finn. Hard. "You care about her."

"Yes. I do."

Nora pushed off the counter. "Then maybe she'll talk to you. She sure as hell isn't talking to me or Allie about whatever's going on with her."

She sounded more disappointed than anything else. Finn would bet money Nora would never admit it.

"Any idea why she's not?" Finn asked, still trying to sound gentle. She wouldn't spill Vivi's secrets, but she could maybe encourage Nora to perceive the situation differently if she had it twisted. Or Finn was giving herself too much credit. In town for five minutes and fixing longstanding issues for everyone? That was a movie plot, not reality.

Nora made a wry face. "Will would say I don't want to let her make her own mistakes."

Bless Will. "What would you say?"

If Finn had to tell someone about this conversation later, she'd mark this as the moment she met Nora the person instead of Nora the defender. Nora's eyes went from guarded to... lost, maybe. "I'd say I'm not any better at being her sister than I was as a substitute mom. I never know what the hell I'm doing."

Either it was more than Nora had meant to reveal to a stranger or she'd exhausted her store of social energy, because without another word she strode off into the back room.

Turquoise-haired Oliver emerged through the curtain, tying on his apron. "You have everything you need?" His eyes flicked around the cafe for his favorite customer. The gal was in the corner, same as last time, her eyes glued to her laptop screen.

Finn held up the coffee. "I'm all set. A piece of free advice, though? There are no guarantees, but you can talk yourself out of trying for a good thing." After all Hollis had done for her, she could at least spread the benefits of his wisdom. That Finn had, uh, ignored.

Oliver stared at Finn, worrying at his lip ring with his teeth. "Yeah," he said thoughtfully. "Maybe you're not wrong."

The bells jangled again—Finn was gonna talk to Will about those things—and when she turned, she saw Vivi walking in.

Vivi smiled at her, and in that moment, Finn knew everything was going to be okay somehow. She had Vivi. She would get a job. It probably wouldn't be in a fancy office, but it would be something, and Finn would work her backside off to turn something into enough.

"Can you get your drink to go?" Vivi closed the distance between them. "I'm sorry, but I want to go home. Oh, hang on. I know why I'm dressed up. Why are you dressed up?"

Finn had watched Vivi get dressed that morning for her off-site educational seminar, and had savored her first-ever view of Vivi in a dress. It was a light pink wrap thing which she'd paired with knee-high black boots. The pre-getting-dressed part had been pretty damn appealing too, when Vivi had been in only a matching bra and panties. Satin and lace, all of it ivory. Finn had repaid that particular kindness by replacing Vivi's nail polish before it could chip. Finn's girl had been delighted to discover that free manicures and pedicures would now be part of her life.

"Eh. Had an interview."

Vivi glanced up at Finn's face, and her expression softened. "Have to start somewhere, right? More importantly, you look hot as hell."

That did ease the disappointment, but a loud crash from the back room kept Finn from saying anything back.

"I'm all right!" Will yelled from the past the curtain.

Oliver looked uncertain. "Should I go check?"

Vivi scrunched up her nose and nodded.

"I'll be right back." He ducked through the curtain.

When he reappeared minutes later with a to-go cup, Nora reemerged as well. She had her arms crossed, but her looming seemed friendlier than before.

Vivi gave Finn her keys as they left.

"You sure?"

"Completely," Vivi said with a satisfied grin.

Finn had to move Vivi's seat back so her knees weren't almost in the steering wheel. Vivi closed her eyes and rested in the passenger seat while Finn drove them back to the apartment, Latin pop playing on the stereo. There were far worse things than driving her girlfriend home, both of them dressed up fancy, and being all mannered as she let Vivi in the front door.

All Vivi could manage for lunch was more oatmeal. She walked Finn through how to make it, since she was fading fast. She tolerated some almond butter mixed into it and she drank plenty of water, so Finn thought they'd done pretty well. Vivi settled on the couch and Finn sat on the coffee table so she could keep looking at the girl. Her girl.

"I forgot," Vivi groaned. "I got you something. Where's my purse?"

Finn got it for her. Making Vivi laugh, bringing her tissues, and retrieving her purse sounded like a fine life to Finn. Vivi rummaged in the purse and pulled out a small brown paper envelope. She handed it to Finn with a flourish. Finn fished around in it and pulled out a hard metal shape.

A key.

Finn wasn't moving in, not yet. Not until she could pay her own way and hopefully then some, and had squared things with Hollis and Ilsa too. Rather than arguing, however, she took Vivi's hand and kissed it.

She could do that now, any time they wanted.

Vivi yawned, and tried to apologize while she yawned, but it was a huge yawn.

Finn laughed. "Do you need an afternoon nap?"

"No, I'm fine! I should tell you this." Vivi yawned again. "I had a video chat in my car with Vicente when I got done with training a bit early. I can't get him to say what he would prefer me to do, he keeps saying it's my choice. He did admit it's hard thinking about not raising his first child himself, especially with me not being Latina, and my Spanish isn't where it should be even for work. I'm terrible at languages."

Finn took a minute to sit with that, and judging by Vivi's serious expression, Vivi was doing the same. It would be a loss for Vicente nobody could ever fix. Plus, if Vivi went forward with it, she'd be raising a little biracial person without Vicente being there day in and day out to help the kid figure out how to deal with racist bullshit.

"You'd have to up your game, wouldn't you?" Finn stroked Vivi's fingers with her thumb. "I'm assuming your stepmom would be around a lot, but it's not the same."

Vivi nodded. "Also not the same, but Austin ISD has Spanish-English dual-language immersion starting in kindergarten. I looked it up and Vicente seemed happier to know that. Happier when I said it might be us, actually. Both of us queer, I mean."

Their eyes met. Finn smiled encouragingly. She might not know the future, but she knew right now, and right now *us* was one of the best words.

Vivi sighed. "He did say he'd sign whatever I needed for custody, if that's what I want. He'd want to visit periodically, so hopefully they wouldn't fuck him over at the border. Maybe have the child visit, too, when they're old enough, so they'd know where they come from."

Finn curled her hand more securely around Vivi's. She didn't want to jump to conclusions. She didn't have a conclusion she wanted to jump to. All she wanted was for Vivi to be able to make a decision and get out from under the stress.

"I called Planned Parenthood," Vivi said. "I didn't know what I'd say until they answered. I ended up asking if they needed volunteer nurses. Because... they would have been there for me. If an abortion was the right choice for me right now. It's not. So I want to help them be there for someone else instead."

Finn was twenty-five years old. She'd gotten one interview, so she could get another, and then another, as many as it took. Vivi was twenty-eight and had a job, an apartment, and a car. A whole lot of people made it through with a whole lot less. They could figure it out.

However, she suspected Vivi's stepmom was going to flip out that her youngest stepdaughter was pregnant, unmarried, and dating an ex-con. And her dad, *ugh*, who knew what would happen there? Finn wondered how long before Vivi realized.

"What did the clinic say about volunteering?"

"They said yes, absolutely! I can do it for as long as I have... free time."

She was starting to sound shaky. Finn switched seats from the coffee table to the couch and drew Vivi under her arm. They fit together, Vivi's head on her shoulder, their clasped hands resting on Finn's leg.

"I bet they might need other kinds of help too," Finn suggested, "maybe during the same hours they need nurses. I could go with you, and I bet there are also ways for us to upgrade our Spanish. If we do it together we'd have somebody to practice with."

"That would be good," Vivi said. "Especially the Spanish. For... later."

Finn didn't blame Vivi for still being skittish about saying it directly. She'd gone through a lot to get to this point. "I do have one suggestion now that you've decided. Maybe tell Nora first?"

Vivi sighed against Finn's chest. "You're right. She wouldn't show it, but she'd be destroyed if I told Alicia first." Finn felt her tense up. "Oh fuck. You haven't even met Alicia yet. Or my stepmom. The due date is in June and we're not married. She's going to kill me!"

Yep, there it was.

Vivi struggled upright and stared at Finn, eyes pleading. "Can we say we're engaged? Please, Finn. If I tell her we're engaged, she can focus on that instead of the other thing. Nora and Will did theirs at the courthouse, and Alicia and Matt don't want to get married. If we say she can do a wedding after a long engagement, it'll distract her!"

That sounded like a one-way ticket to some kind of terrible blowup down the road, and Finn wasn't going to mess this up. It was going to be tough enough navigating the situation with Vivi's father. Finn shook her head. "Vee, I love you, but I'm not going to lie to your family."

Vivi deflated a bit. "Dammit. You're right. I know you're right. Surely she'll be so excited about her first grandchild she won't care about anything else? I know she'd only flip out because she loves me and wants me to have stability, but it could be a real mess if she does."

Tomorrow, Finn might also suggest Vivi let Nora help break the news. Not because Vivi couldn't do it on her own, mind. Finn had to make that perfectly clear or not say it at all. But Vivi needed somebody on her team, and whether or not Nora was perfect at it, she was her baby sister's defender.

"Promise me you'll meet them soon?" Vivi asked. "Allie and Matt, and my stepmom? She's going to love you, I promise. She loves people with a sense of humor. I don't know what to do about my dad. You have your mom, so you get it, right?"

"I'll meet whoever you want me to meet. Looking forward to it."

Vivi tried to say something else, but lost it in a yawn.

Finn squeezed her hand. "Go take a nap, sweetheart."

"You'll be here when I wake up?"

"Of course." Where else would she rather be?

Vivi got to her feet, but stopped, her eyes going wide. "Oh wow. It's New Year's Eve. Are we doing anything? Do you usually do anything, do you have any traditions? I mean, did you before?"

Before being locked up. Before getting herself stuck in a miserable, scary place, where she had met Vivi. Would Finn go back and do crime and incarceration over again to make that happen? It depended on how time travel worked. If her rerouted self would never know what she missed, maybe. If she'd wake up every morning thinking she could have had Vivi, no way.

"I've never been in the habit of going out on New Year's Eve," Finn confessed. "Too many drunk drivers and whatever. We could do something here." An idea struck her. "Hey, did you ever watch The Legend of Korra after Avatar? I've heard positive things about it."

Vivi covered her mouth with both hands.

Oh no. "What? Is it bad?"

Vivi dropped her hands enough to speak. "I never finished Avatar."

That was insupportable. "Vivienne Curiel, I love you but I am appalled by your behavior."

"I'm sorry!" Vivi waved her hands helplessly. "It made me too sad to watch it when I couldn't talk to you about it!"

Was this how Vivi would get out of trouble in the future? Be all cute and tug on Finn's heartstrings?

Finn could easily live with it.

"Go sleep," she said. "When you get up, we'll have dinner and an Avatar marathon."

Vivi beamed. "If I fall asleep before midnight, you'll wake me up, right? Promise? I want to do the kiss when the clock strikes thing."

Finn could live with that too.

CHAPTER FOURTEEN

"Vee? Wake up, honey." Finn hated to rouse her. Vivi had only made it through three episodes after dinner before she'd dozed off again, tucked into Finn's side, her body growing heavier and heavier as she relaxed and drifted into sleep.

Now she stirred on Finn's shoulder and made a tiny, adorable noise of protest.

"It's New Year's Eve," Finn whispered, "and it's two minutes to midnight."

Vivi jumped and shook herself a little. "What? That's not — I need to brush my teeth!" She scrambled up and out from under the blanket Finn had draped across her and dashed for the bathroom.

Finn simply took a sip of water. They'd eaten plain pasta and a side of chickpeas for dinner, after all, and she hadn't been the one asleep.

When Vivi raced back out to the couch and sat down, Finn smelled her raspberry icing lip balm again. She held up Vivi's phone. "Ten," she said, reading from the countdown clock Vivi had installed during dinner.

"Nine," Vivi said. "Eight. Seven."

"Six." Finn imagined kissing her. "Five. Four. Three."

"Two." Vivi leaned closer. "One."

As the countdown app played the first few notes of Auld Lang Syne and Finn heard someone setting off firecrackers outside, she and Vivi kissed. It was soft and cute, and Vivi giggled against Finn's mouth. Finn found she quite liked the sensation.

"I love you," Vivi whispered as she pulled back. Finn chased her for one more kiss, and another, and Vivi laughed again and gave them to her, until it was pretty clear they'd end up somewhere other than on the couch. Or not. Either way.

Vivi's phone rang.

They both startled and looked to where Finn had laid it on the coffee table. Then Finn turned back to Vivi, confused. Who the heck would call after midnight on New Year's Eve? Unless it was an emergency.

Vivi reached for the phone, but Finn was quicker in handing it to her. As it rang the second time, Vivi said, "It's Alicia," before answering. "Allie, are you okay?"

The voice on the other end was loud enough for Finn to hear the words. "Happy New Yeaaaaarrrr! You are *such* a good sister. Matt! She is such a good sister, tell her!"

The male voice was more indistinct at first, but definitely laughter. It got more clear, as if maybe Matt had grabbed the phone. "Sorry Vivi! She's completely trashed, it's hilarious."

Vivi stared at Finn while she pulled the phone further from her ear, her eyes wide with either shock or horror. Finn did her best to keep a straight face. She *had* agreed to meet Alicia and Matt. She simply hadn't anticipated it would happen so soon and under such circumstances. If there was a more opposite experience from meeting Nora than this, Finn couldn't imagine it.

Alicia was lodging some kind of objection in the background, and suddenly there was a noise and Matt yelled. Then there was a scuffling sound as if the phone had been dropped.

Vivi covered the speaker as peals of laughter from both her sister and her sister's partner erupted from her phone. "I am so, so sorry. They are not normally like this. I mean, they go to parties and they drink, but wow."

Finn covered her mouth to hide how much she was about to crack up.

"Sorry," Matt said, somewhat breathless. "She knocked over a glass of ice water in my lap. No, Allie, let go, we're going to hang up n—"

"Heyyyy!" Alicia objected. She'd gotten the phone back or at least gotten her mouth near it. She spoke in an exaggerated hush like she thought she was being sneaky. "Vivi, I met this hot woman earlier, and she and her special person do the open thing too, and I'm totally gonna do her next weekend. I'm gonna go over to her apartment and take all my clothes off and it's gonna be *awesome.*"

Even if someone had offered to pay her enough to send Vivi's baby to Harvard for four years, Finn could not have held back from busting out laughing. Vivi covered her face with her free hand.

"Who's that?" Alicia yelled enthusiastically, and Vivi flinched away from the phone. "Your hot butch girlfriend? Finn? Hi Finn! Vivi got so drunk after she got fired and she couldn't stop talking about you, did she tell you?"

Vivi dropped her hand, and Finn could tell horror was overcoming shock. "Matt?" Vivi called. "Where *are* you?"

"At a friend's house," Matt said reassuringly in the background. "It's okay, she's not taking her clothes off with anybody tonight. I've only had a couple of mimosas and they took everyone's keys when we got here anyway. We're staying over. Love you, talk to you tomorrow."

"I love you too," Alicia said more loudly, her words falling over each other now. "I love you *so* much Vivienne, and Finn the hot butch girlfriend I know I'm going to love you too, but not as much as my sisters because sisters are for *life*!"

Not always true, but it was a nice sentiment. Vivi obviously felt the same, judging by her fond smile. "I love you too, Allie."

"Now I'm gonna call *Nora*," Alicia pronounced solemnly, and Finn only heard the beginning of Matt's objection before the call disconnected.

Vivi put her phone back on the coffee table. If Finn were a better person, she'd have been less amused at the idea of Nora getting that call. She also wouldn't so desperately want a recording of it.

"So," Finn finally offered. "Are we partying with them next weekend?"

Vivi clapped her hand over her mouth, but it was too late. She choked back a laugh, coughed, and started to laugh for real, her other hand reaching out for Finn's.

Finn took it, folded it up in her own, and waited for Vivi's peals of laughter to subside into giggles and then a couple of deep clearing breaths.

"No thank you." Vivi wiped her eyes with her free hand. "I am totally fine with them living their lives exactly how they want to since they're not hurting anybody, but no. I'm good."

Finn couldn't help smiling. "You're more of a cartoons on the couch kind of girl?"

Vivi grinned back. "I can think of better things to do on the couch."

They didn't do many of those better things on the couch. They tried. They got interrupted a second time by a text, this one from Nora: Alicia's name and six eyerolling emoji, which surprised and delighted Finn because she wouldn't have guessed Nora used emoji. By that point, they both had to admit the spontaneity was gone and they might as well move to the bed to be more comfortable.

Comfortable meant room to kiss Vivi anywhere without fear of falling off the couch. Comfortable meant the nightstand was close by, with dental dams in the drawer, and plenty of space to get under the sheets and between Vivi's thighs.

Finn was a big fan of comfortable.

Vivi was a big fan of Finn's lucky rainbow sports bra.

They talked afterwards, about Hollis's accident and Ilsa's divorce. Finn had to distract Vivi from getting out of bed to start making a list of community resources she wanted to research.

Finn collected their phones from the living room and got them plugged in—well, got Vivi's plugged in, as Finn's rarely needed charging—while Vivi went to brush her teeth yet again. Her dedication to dental hygiene was impressive. They snuggled up together, Vivi's head on Finn's shoulder. Movies made lying down together look a lot easier; in real life, somebody's extra arm never had a logical place to go.

"I thought I might tell Nora tomorrow," Vivi said quietly. "Knockdown's closed, so she'll probably be out in a park or something. Would you come with me? Not, like, to be right there when I tell her, but close by."

"Sure. No problem." She'd be wherever Vivi wanted her to be.

Finn didn't remember falling asleep, but noise woke her up. A buzz. Her phone. She fumbled for it in the dim light of morning, rolling slightly away from Vivi. Sometime in the night they'd unentangled from each other, but they were both still in the middle of the bed, tucked together close.

Finn checked the screen. A text.

I hope this doesn't wake you. This is Dustin Choi. Happy New Year! This is my cell, please text back whenever you get up. We'd like to offer you the position if you can start training tomorrow.

She blinked. She read it four times and it said the same thing every time. A full-time job. With health insurance and paid time off for when her medicines betrayed her, and—Finn had to stop for a second and process—the possibility of paying rent.

"Is everything okay?" Vivi asked drowsily. "Was that Hollis?"

"Yeah," Finn said instinctively, dazed. "No, sorry, it wasn't Hollis, but yes everything's okay."

Better than okay. Better than she'd had any right to expect. Ridiculous luck, struck-by-lightning luck.

Hell if she was going to complain. She should get up and call Dr. Choi back. She should get her butt to Target and Old Navy to get a work wardrobe if they were open today.

"Vee?"

"Mmmyeah?" Vivi slung her arm across Finn's chest and nuzzled her face into Finn's shoulder. Her hair was splayed every which way, some of it in her face, and she hadn't even opened her eyes yet. Adorable.

Maybe the big news could keep. "I've got a few gift cards, need to get some clothes. You wanna help pick 'em?"

Vivi hummed happily. "Oooh, shopping. Sure. Gimme five more minutes."

Two minutes later, her breathing was so regular that Finn knew she'd fallen back to sleep. Finn sent Dr. Choi back a quick text, and waited for his confirmation text before she herself started breathing again.

She started a new job tomorrow. Entire social media platforms had been launched, succeeded, collapsed, and died since the last time she'd started a new job. New jobs meant new people, new skills, and for her in this case, no payment handling for at least six months.

That was tomorrow, though. Today, right now, she had Vivi. Beautiful, compassionate, often righteously indignant in the best way. It was light enough now for Finn to see her clearly. After all their time together, Finn would have sworn she could describe Vivi in detail, but she would have missed so many small things. There was a very faint mark on her nose Finn suspected was an old failed piercing. Her hairline wasn't exactly symmetrical; the right side arched slightly higher.

Finn was finally getting a chance to love her up close, instead of from a distance.

That, Finn knew she could get right.

EPILOGUE

Finn pulled Vivi's car into a parking spot as close to the basketball court as she could find and turned off the engine. Even from here, Finn could tell which player was Nora. She dribbled down the court, her long ponytail swinging behind her. Finn wondered if she might give Nora a run for her money once she'd had a chance to dust off her high school team skills, but decided not to bring that up anytime soon, and took off her seat belt.

She didn't hear Vivi taking off her own seat belt. Finn looked over. Vivi was in those curve-hugging jeans again, a tight cream-colored t-shirt with a big rainbow heart in the middle of it, and pink sneakers. She'd done her hair in two braids that hung down in front of her shoulders. She was overwhelmingly adorable. She was also worrying at her lower lip with her teeth.

"You don't have to do this," Finn reminded her.

"Then I'd have to come up with another explanation for Nora of why I called and wanted to talk today."

"You could tell her I got the job."

Vivi wrinkled her nose. "I could have told her that over

the phone. It's okay. I'm going to get it over with, and then we can go shopping." She reached over and unbuckled the seat belt, letting it retract slowly. "We're still going shopping after, right?"

Finn smiled, caught Vivi's hand, and brought it to her lips for a quick kiss. "Whatever you want, sweetheart."

After a deep sigh, Vivi let go and got out of the car. Finn cracked her door and pushed it open, stood up, and searched for a place she could hang out to be nearby, but not too close because this was Vivi's thing. A green park bench sat not too far from the car, between the parking lot and the court. Perfect. Finn settled down on it as Vivi kept walking. Vivi stopped when she got to the chain-link fence, on the other end of the court from where Nora was executing a gorgeous bank shot.

You know, you might end up being friends with that gal.

It was something to consider, anyway.

The players broke for water. Vivi waved to Nora, who gave one wave back and then loped across the court to the gate near where her sister was waiting. Finn watched Nora fiddle with the latch, hoping desperately Vivi was going to get what she needed from this.

As Nora closed the gate behind her, Vivi was already wrapping her arms around herself. They both took a few steps away from the gate into the grass that started where the side-walk left off. Vivi started to talk. Nora's hands went up like she was going to put them over her mouth, or on top of her head in disbelief or frustration…

And then she lunged at Vivi, grabbing her up in a hug that almost knocked her over.

Finn had to admit, she wiped away a couple of tears as Nora kissed the top of Vivi's head. Vivi was bawling, unsur-prisingly, but laughing too, and Nora hugged her again, lifting her up until only her toes brushed the ground and Vivi made some kind of halfhearted protest. Finally Nora put her down, and they exchanged probably two more sentences before the basketball crew was calling Nora to come back. She glanced back to them before looking back to her sister.

Vivi gestured for Nora to go back, wiping her face. Nora tugged one of Vivi's braids playfully and then walked backwards to the gate. Finn now had proof that the woman smiled, truly smiled, and it was a damn fine sight.

Right before Nora swung the gate shut behind her, she looked at Finn and raised one hand in greeting. Finn raised her own, and Nora nodded, appearing satisfied, before going back to her friends.

Vivi watched Nora until the game picked back up, then looked skyward. She put one hand to her lips and blew a kiss. Finn wiped away a couple more tears hastily before Vivi ambled back to the bench.

"Sooo," Finn said as if she didn't just watch the whole scene, "did it go well?"

Vivi grinned. "Yes, you goof. She said she'd come with me to tell our parents, too, if I want."

"Do you want her to?"

A warning shout went up from the basketball game, and they both glanced over. Nora was on the ground, but she was already waving off offered hands and getting back up.

"She's pretty tough," Vivi said. "Maybe it'd be a good idea to stand, like, not *right* behind her? But kinda tucked in a little bit. Just in case."

Finn nodded. "Excellent plan. First, though, I suppose we have some other life stuff to get done."

"Sounds absolutely wonderful," Vivi agreed, taking Finn's hand and pulling her gently back towards the car. "Let's get started."

THANKS SO MUCH FOR READING!

If you liked this story, please consider leaving even a brief review on Amazon and Goodreads! Reviews are authors' love language.

You can also keep reading for a preview of the next Love at Knockdown book, **Shake Things Up**, where Vivi's sister Alicia meets a damsel in distress under surprising circumstances.

Want more queer romance?

Follow me on Goodreads, Amazon, or Twitter, or sign up for my e-newsletter for a **FREE short story** about how Will and Nora met, plus updates on future Love at Knockdown stories and my other contemporary, sci-fi, and hopepunk queer romances:

SkyeWritesRomance.com

I write…

- F/F, F/M with queer main characters, and sometimes M/M starring bi/pan guys
- anything from from fluffy to angsty and even suspense
- sometimes monogamy, other times polyamory

...and some of it might be perfect for you.

ACKNOWLEDGMENTS

My sincere thanks to editor Suzanne Lahna of The Quick Fox and all the beta readers who helped with this story, including folks from the Cactusland writing group. Special thanks to JP, this story's most amazing cheerleader. I couldn't have done this without y'all.

ABOUT THE AUTHOR

I write a variety of queer romance, both contemporary and science fiction, that's sometimes about polyamorous relationships.

I'm bi, my pronouns are she/her, and I currently live in Austin, Texas because of all the libraries and breakfast tacos.

For more stories and updates:
SkyeWritesRomance.com

SNEAK PREVIEW

Love at Knockdown Book 2: Shake Things Up

The ten minute conference call invite should have been a dead giveaway that Noelle was being laid off. Ten minutes turned out to be just long enough for the CEO and CFO to say a few buzzwords like "rightsizing" and "refocusing" while Noelle blinked and tried to process. After eight months working pre-dawn to post-dusk, her job as the organize-everything generalist at this startup was gone.

Now here she was, opening her trunk to remove the cardboard box full of the contents of her desk and carry it into her apartment. She'd never been laid off before. She'd relocated to Austin for this job. She hadn't been unemployed since she turned thirteen and started babysitting half her life ago!

Okay. Yeah. She was a little shaky.

Noelle took a deep calming breath, closed the trunk, and decided to just… deal. Between her mentor making calls and her own connections, this would sort itself out. Her health insurance would last another 27 days. Garland had been a fantastic boyfriend to let her crash with him after her rental condo got sold three months ago. She'd meant to look for a new place, but she hadn't yet had time. So, she had a roof over her head a healthy bank balance. Everything was going to be fine.

Music was playing behind his apartment door as she approached. Garland must have made it home early somehow. Maybe they could… go out? Talk over dinner. Maybe go completely wild and catch a movie? When was the last time they'd managed an actual date around their work schedules?

She almost stopped in her tracks when her brain supplied the answer: New Year's Eve. Over two months ago.

Noelle Davenport, what the hell? Maybe this layoff was a wakeup call. Career success was great, but she'd let things get a bit out of hand.

Propping her box on one hip, she unlocked the door. She pushed it open, bumped it closed behind her, and took the three steps down the entry hall which brought her to the living room.

Wherein she saw two half-full glasses of red wine on the coffee table and Garland scrambling off the couch while frantically trying to rebutton his dress shirt. A woman with long dark hair sat on that same couch, grey sleeveless dress rucked up to show bright purple underwear.

The woman was staring not at Noelle, but up at Garland. She looked pissed.

And something in Noelle's heart… crumpled.

"Noelle," Garland said, sounding as if he actually cared, "I can explain."

"Garland," the woman said coldly, "shut the fuck up."

Noelle suddenly realized she wasn't breathing and tried to start again. She got one inhale but she'd pulled the box so tight against herself there wasn't much room for her chest to expand. She couldn't figure out how to fix it.

The woman got up and tugged down her dress. She was

sexy as hell, Noelle realized, which was the most bizarre thing to notice, but it was true. Great calves, an hourglass shape, a few inches taller than Noelle. If Noelle and Garland had seen her in public, one of them would have nudged the other. A little harmless lady-appreciating from a bi gal and her straight boyfriend. Garland had always enjoyed appreciating.

Oh fuck. Was this the first time he'd done this?

"I take it," the woman said to Noelle, much more gently, "that you are Garland's girlfriend, but not the woman I spoke with on the phone who said it would be okay to fuck him. I'm so sorry."

Noelle didn't know whether to nod or shake her head. She wasn't entirely certain she could speak. The woman who had been making out with Garland was angry. Noelle wanted to be angry. If she were, it wouldn't sting so badly.

The woman turned to Garland. "Is her name even Noelle, you unbelievable piece of shit?"

Her question seemed to snap Garland out of his panicked staring. "Look, Alicia, this is between me and Noelle, so you can just—"

The next few things seemed to happen all in a jumble. Garland took a couple of steps towards Noelle. Noelle's back hit the wall as she dropped the box.

And Alicia practically knocked over the coffee table getting between Garland and Noelle.

"Whatever the fuck you think you're about to do, think again," she said to him in a low voice. "Noelle, is it okay if I tell your scumbag cheating soon-to-be-ex-boyfriend to get the hell out of here?"

Noelle hadn't believed Garland was going to hurt her. She simply hadn't wanted him to touch her. He'd been all over somebody else not five minutes ago.

That somebody else had run to protect Noelle.

"It's my apartment!" Garland objected. "She hasn't been paying rent!"

She didn't want to cry in front of her… not boyfriend. Ex-boyfriend. The guy she'd had fantastic morning sex with yesterday. She just wanted all of this to stop. "Please go."

"Noelle, baby, come on, we can talk about this—"

"Did you not fucking hear her?" the woman shielding Noelle demanded. "And do you see any conceivable way you're the good guy in this situation?"

Garland's expression wavered. "Fine," he said to Noelle, then shot a resentful glance at Alicia. "But you and your stuff better be gone when I get back at midnight. Shouldn't be too hard. You were barely here anyway."

He stalked over to the entertainment center and yanked his phone out of the docking station, killing the music, which Noelle hadn't realized was still playing. He slammed the door behind him.

Everything was quiet.

Noelle watched Alicia take a long, deep breath and shake out her hands before turning around. Her manicure matched her underwear. Another detail Noelle shouldn't be aware of. How was any of this happening?

"I am so fucking sorry," Alicia said. "I'll go. I mean, I wouldn't say no to borrowing your bathroom first and using whatever mouthwash you have. Or, like, vodka would work. Something to kill the gross germs."

Noelle swallowed, nodded, and managed to gesture in the direction of the hallway that led to their bedroom and bathroom. No, Garland's bedroom and bathroom. As he'd reminded her so pointedly, she'd only ever been a guest here.

"Thank you. Oh, and you can call me Allie."

When she'd strode off down the hall and closed the bathroom door behind her, Noelle let herself slide slowly down the wall until her legs splayed out in front of her. She hadn't cried in front of Garland. The box of her office things was another matter entirely.

Thank fuck there was mouthwash. Allie poured some into her cupped hand and slurped it up. Undignified, sure, but better than getting caught with her dress hiked up to her waist with a two-timing fuckwit jackwagon like Garland Whitmore.

She was never, ever, ever hooking up with a partnered stranger again unless she talked to their partner in person and, like, cross-checked with two of their social media channels or something. *She's traveling on business and the internet connection at her hotel is shit, what about a phone call?*

He! Was! Such! A! Tool!

Allie rinsed out her mouth and washed her face, hands, and throat for good measure. If only she'd snagged her purse on the way to the bathroom so she could call Matt. He was in their apartment not five miles away, playing video games and keeping an ear out for his phone in case of an emergency. Surely this counted as an emergency.

Although, dialing the hyperbole back, it was more of an emergency for Noelle. Who was really fucking pretty. Allie would have hit on Noelle before Garland if she'd seen them both at a party. Chin-length blond hair, a slight build, and her cup-sleeve blouse was trim enough to show off her pretty little breasts. Yes, Allie could be simultaneously aware that Noelle had gotten fucked over and that she had nice tits.

How disappointing that Allie had met Garland online first. She had not expected to end up in a stranger's bathroom sluicing water off herself and blotting with tissues because she didn't want to use a towel he might have touched.

Noelle's eyes had gone so big when she walked in. Allie had waited for her to start screaming, crying, something. Nothing. It honestly made Allie a bit worried. If Noelle had started spitting fire it would have been more reassuring.

When Allie stepped back down the hall, she could see Noelle had ended up on the floor, legs out in front of her. Not good.

Allie slowed down and tried to make noise with her bare feet so Noelle knew she was approaching. Her pumps were… somewhere. Noelle glanced up when Allie got close, and her eyes were wet.

"Hey," Allie said, trying to sound super-nice and super-gentle and super-not-like the woman who'd been playing grownup games with Noelle's boyfriend on their couch.

"Hey," Noelle said back. She sounded exhausted.

Allie should probably go? Say sorry again and get out of the poor girl's face, give her the space to call her mom or best friend or sibling to vent and figure out next steps?

Nora or Vivi would know what to do. Both of Allie's sisters were effective people managers in their own ways, a skill that had skipped Allie. She might be a living stereotype for an actuary with degrees in math and accounting, but she could be real about her strengths. Her specialties were numbers, partying, and sex, in that order. Feelings stuff was Matt's department in their relationship.

But Allie was the only one here. "Is it okay if I sit down?" At least she could stop making Noelle crane her neck.

Noelle blinked a couple of times, wiped a few tears out of her eyes. "Sure."

Allie folded her legs under her as she sat, trying not to flash poor Noelle with anything more than she'd already seen. "So was he lying about it being his place? Do you need to get out in the next, like, six hours?"

"He wasn't lying. Honestly I'm tempted to just walk out the door and start driving. Today's been..."

That kind of thinking wasn't going to make Allie feel okay leaving. "Here's the way I see it. We've already skipped the part of the script where you start screaming at me for homewrecking. The pop culture script would say so."

Noelle managed to smile a bit.

Good. "So, I don't see any reason why you have to do the bit where you're cast out into the cold with only the clothes on your back because your man was unfaithful."

Noelle smiled a little more. "I'm from Chicago. It's never cold here."

"What are you talking about? February is scarf month." Allie took a second to consider what any of the competent people in her life would do. Channeling Nora was probably the most helpful. Safety first. "Do we need to worry about what happens if he comes back before midnight?"

Noelle looked startled. "No, sorry. I just really didn't want him to touch me after— shit, I sound horrible. I'm sure you're a very nice person."

When nice was called for, sure. "You're fine, no worries. I kinda want a shower myself." Which sounded like Allie was making it about her. Fuck. "Again, I am so sorry. I would never in a zillion years have tried to get with him if I had any idea. My partner and I do the open thing but we don't lie."

Noelle nodded slowly. "That is so completely different from what he did."

Truer words might never have been spoken. "Well, at least you have one box to start with."

"It's full of my stuff from work. I got home so early because I got laid off."

Well fuck. This cluster was not Allie's fault, except maybe she'd been a little too trusting, but damn she felt even worse now. Allie might have taken a woe-is-me break in the bathroom earlier, but she did have a handle on who'd had the more awful day between the two of them.

Noelle brought her hands up to rub her face, pushed her hair back. She had pretty eyes too, light brown. "It's okay. I've only been here for a few months anyway, so most of my stuff is in storage."

She looked so tired.

"Need help packing?"

Matt almost had it. He was so close! But when Allie's ring-tone sounded, he abandoned all hope of finishing the map of his current level in Etrian Odyssey. The call probably wasn't about a safety issue. Probably he'd have to put his pants back on and meet her somewhere for dessert to cheer her up about a bad lay.

He seriously did not want to put on pants.

He accepted the call anyway, of course, because there was always a chance it was a safety thing. "Whatcha need, babe?"

"I might not be home until late because I'm helping Noelle pack so she can move out. Not the Noelle I talked to on the phone, the real one. Garland's a cheater."

What?

"I know," Allie said, because living together since college did lend itself to them reading each other's minds sometimes. "Total catastrophe, but I offered to help box up her shit and get most of it to her storage unit. She needed a drink so I fixed her one and told her to point to which things are hers."

Allie wasn't ungenerous, but she usually had to be told

how to help people. She didn't volunteer. If Matt had put the picture together right, the guy whose photo and contact info Matt had in an email from Allie had not cleared his date with his girlfriend. Surely the woman hadn't then asked Allie to help her move? "Who are you and what have you done with my partner?"

"Shut it, loser."

That sounded more like the gal he knew. "Excellent, you haven't been replaced by an alien. I'm slightly confused but I'm proud of you. Are you sure y'all are safe? Do you want me to come over?"

"Noelle says we're cool. I'll tell you the whole story later, but her storage unit is up on 183 near the Spicewood Springs exit, so I don't know how long it's going to take."

As long as she was safe and Matt didn't have to put pants on, she could be as late as she wanted. Tomorrow was Saturday and it wasn't his turn for a shift at pediatric urgent care. "Thanks for the heads up. Is whoever she's crashing with already home? If not, you could offer to take her out to dinner while she waits."

Dead silence. Fairly typical when Alicia Curiel felt embarrassed.

"You don't know where she's going to stay, do you?"

"Was I supposed to ask?"

She sounded a little frustrated. Interesting. Normally she wouldn't have been bothered.

"You don't have to ask," Matt reassured her, "and she may not want to tell you. However, if she doesn't have anywhere to stay tonight, you could offer her our guest room, you know? We could do the same as with hookups, we all exchange info and she sends ours to somebody. Y'all could meet me at Knockdown and we could all hang out for a while first, see if she's okay with it."

"If you show up without pants I am locking you out."

Matt choked back a laugh. "Have I ever gone out in public without pants?" He liked to be comfortable; it didn't make him an exhibitionist.

"I'm getting ready for the day you try. Anyway, sure, I'll ask her if she has someplace to go. Hopefully she doesn't decide I'm a serial killer."

"Maybe ask her *after* you get her things into storage." If this Noelle had accepted Allie's help rather than calling someone who hadn't just slept with her boyfriend, she might not have anybody else to call. It would be a shame to spook her and leave her all alone with that project.

"Okay. Thanks Matt. I guess you're useful for something besides healing sick children."

"I wish I'd recorded that so I could play it back tomorrow when you're whining at me about making French toast."

"Maybe I wouldn't have to whine if you'd get up at a reasonable hour and make it. Ever think of that?"

"Go help your new friend, favorite girl."

"Go finish your dungeon map, favorite guy." She disconnected the call.

Well. This certainly wasn't the evening he'd expected when Allie told him about her date plans. Granted, it had been morning at the time, which meant he'd been in the shower and all he could think about was the coffee she was handing him in the travel mug. Too much water splashed into it in a normal mug and Allie always fussed anyway that he was going to break the ceramic and cut himself. Given his usual level of consciousness at six a.m., she probably wasn't wrong.

Matt put his phone back on the coffee table and picked up the video game controller again. Then he put it back down. He wouldn't be able to concentrate now; he'd be worried about Allie. He glanced at his phone again, wondering whether he should go get dressed just in case.

Or he could open up the dating app again, just to browse. They were a week away from leaving on their road trip to Denver for three days of music at Red Rocks. There were guys in Denver using the app. He'd checked. Several times.

Talking to a guy before the trip made him a little nervous, however, like he was getting ahead of himself. Matt didn't even know if what he'd started considering about himself in the past six months or so was real. Wouldn't he know already if he was anything other than straight? There were queer people all around him. He'd been with Allie for ten years and she'd been tumbling people of all genders all that time. Her sister Vivi was pan too, and their oldest sister Nora had shacked up with a queer guy, Will.

Will was kind of the problem. Not that Matt had a thing for Will. It was listening to Will talk about guys. What he said sounded awfully similar to things that ran through Matt's head sometimes. Things Matt had always kind of... discounted. Which maybe he was leaning towards not doing anymore.

Actually planning to meet up with a specific guy in Denver, though?

Matt picked up his controller again and waited to see if Allie would call back.

Sign up for my newsletter for updates about Noelle, Allie, and Matt's story:

SkyeWritesRomance.com

Printed in Great Britain
by Amazon